"You Know *Nothing* About Me, Sam," Kiera Said, The Fire In Her Eyes Turning To Ice ...thing."

"That's the understate......................." Sam's hands tightened .... sharply aw......................................away.

"Where do .... yelled after her.

"I'm leaving.' ....im a cool glance over her shoulder. "Don ....orry, I'll take the back way so no one will see me."

He started after her, swore, then stopped, raked a hand through his hair.

No woman had ever made him feel helpless like this before. Made him feel out of control like this. He didn't like it. Not one damn bit.

So he made no attempt to stop her.

But long after she was gone, the taste of her lingered in his mouth. He drowned it with a bottle of Scotch and cursed the day she'd walked into his hotel.

Dear Reader,

The ingredients for my October Silhouette Desire novel
are food, scandal and a big helping of spicy sex! I had
a great time writing Kiera and Sam's story, and I loved
returning to Wolf River to check up on characters from
previous books. You might remember Sam from
Miss Pruitt's Private Life. He was the hunky hotel
manager who made Evan so incredibly jealous when he
took Marcy out for drinks. I knew Sam would have to
have his own story and sure enough, Kiera showed up,
and I just needed to step back and let them talk.

Of course, they did a lot more than talk….

There's plenty of heat in this kitchen. These two just
need to watch out they don't get burned!

Happy reading!

Barbara McCauley

Come say hello at my Web site,
www.barbaramccauley.com, and check out my recipes!

BARBARA McCAULEY

BLACKHAWK'S BETRAYAL

Silhouette®

Desire

Published by Silhouette Books

America's Publisher of Contemporary Romance

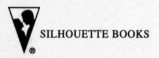

SILHOUETTE BOOKS

ISBN-13: 978-0-373-76754-0
ISBN-10:   0-373-76754-4

BLACKHAWK'S BETRAYAL

Copyright © 2006 by Barbara Joel

Visit Silhouette Books at www.eHarlequin.com

Printed in U.S.A.

Titles in Barbara McCauley's SECRETS! series

Silhouette Desire

Silhouette Intimate Moments

Silhouette Books

Blackhawk Legacy

Summer Gold
"A Wolf River Summer"

BARBARA McCAULEY,

who has written more than twenty novels for Silhouette Books, lives in Southern California with her own handsome hero husband, Frank, who makes it easy to believe in and write about the magic of romance. Barbara's stories have won and been nominated for numerous awards, including the prestigious RITA® Award from the Romance Writers of America, Best Desire of the Year from *Romantic Times BOOKclub* and Best Short Contemporary from the National Reader's Choice Awards.

This book is dedicated to Jennifer Stockton, Chef Extraordinaire! Thanks for all your help and expertise, sweetheart. Your secret for chocolate mousse is safe with me.

One

She should be in Paris.

Sighing, Kiera glanced at the yellow-lit dial on her rental car dashboard. Nine thirty-two, Texas time. If she had got on her plane this morning, she would have landed at the Charles de Gaulle Airport two hours ago. At this very moment, she would be checking into her room at the hotel Château Frontenac. Ordering room service. Sipping espresso while she nibbled on a *navettes*. Sinking her exhausted body into a Louis XVI four-poster bed.

Instead, she sat in the cracked asphalt parking lot of Sadie's Shangri-La Motel and Motor Lodge.

Welcome. Park Your Cars Out Front, Your Horses Out Back, flashed the pink neon vacancy sign.

She didn't know whether to laugh or cry, so she dropped her head into her hands and did both.

"Damn you, Trey," she said through clenched teeth. "Damn you, damn you, damn you."

She let herself rant for a full ten seconds, then wiped her tears and flipped the visor down to study her face in the lit mirror. *Scary,* was her first thought—*deal with it,* her second. Mumbling curses again, she dug through her purse and pulled out a compact of cover-up, then carefully blotted the fading bruise beside her left eye. Not perfect, but the best she could do unless she put on her sunglasses, which, considering the fact that it was pitch black outside, just *might* draw attention to herself.

And *that* she certainly didn't want to do.

Adjusting her bangs and the sides of her hair to hide the fading bruise, she stepped out of the car and stretched her stiff muscles. She was too tired to care that her skirt, a pristine white ten hours ago, now looked like tissue paper pulled out of a gift bag. Nor did she care that her sleeveless blouse, a clean, crisp green when she'd left the ranch this morning, currently had the appearance of wilted lettuce.

It is what it is.

A double-trailer big rig rumbled past the motel, jarring her out of her thoughts. She slung her purse strap over her shoulder, sucked in a breath, then made her way to the motel's front office. Heat from the sweltering day lingered, and the humidity clung to her like wet plastic wrap. *Shower,* she thought, drawing the heavy, damp air into her lungs. She needed one desperately. A long one to wash off the grime and sweat of the day's travel.

When she opened the glass door, a buzzer sounded

overhead and the scent of coffee hung heavy in the air. The desk clerk, a well-endowed petite blonde with Texas-size hair, stood behind the counter, hands on her voluptuous hips and her gaze locked on the screen of a small corner television.

"Be right with y'all," the woman said without even glancing up.

Kiera held back the threatening whimper. Born and raised Texan, she knew what "be right with y'all," *really* meant: sometime between the near future and next Christmas.

Living in New York the past three years had made her impatient, she realized. She'd become accustomed to the frantic rush of people, the swell of city traffic, skyscrapers and closed-in spaces. A delicatessen on every corner.

The thought of food reminded her she hadn't eaten today. She'd kill for one of those deli sandwiches right now. A ten-pound ham and cheese, with lettuce and tomatoes and—

"No!"

The shout made Kiera jump back and clutch her purse. The desk clerk threw up her hands in disgust, which set the strands of silver circles on her earlobes swirling.

"I *knew* I couldn't trust those two," she exclaimed, gesturing angrily at the TV. "For eight weeks she carries Brett and Randy's scrawny, lazy asses and what did it get the poor girl? What?"

Kiera wasn't certain if the woman—Mattie, according to the plastic badge on her white polo shirt—really wanted an answer, but she doubted it.

"A boot in her butt, that's what. Lower than manure, that's what those two jerks are." Shaking her head, Mattie grabbed the remote and lowered the volume, then turned and stretched her bright red lips into a smile. "You checking in, honey?"

Kiera hesitated, briefly considered taking her chances that she might find a room at a hotel in town. Someplace not quite so far off the beaten path. Someplace…safer. Then she remembered how much cash she had and shook off her apprehension. "The sign said you had a vacancy."

"Sure do." Mattie moved to a computer monitor behind the counter. "Single or double?"

"Single."

Mattie's long, glossy red nails clicked over the keys. "Kitchenette?"

Kiera didn't really plan on cooking, but, then, she hadn't planned on being here, either. "Sure."

"How long y'all staying?" Mattie asked.

"I—I'm not sure." God, this was a bad idea, she thought. A *really* bad idea. "Maybe a week or so."

"Name?"

Kiera shifted uneasily. She didn't dare use her real name. At least, not her *last* name. "Kiera Daniels."

The desk clerk entered the name into her computer, then printed out a form and slid it across the counter. "Credit card?"

She thought about the name on her credit card, the fact that she could easily be traced back here if she used it, not to mention the fact that the name might raise questions. "I'd, ah, like to pay cash."

Lifting one penciled brow, Mattie glanced up. "I'll need two night's deposit."

"All right." She pulled out her wallet and opened it, felt her heart sink as she remembered most of her money was in *francs,* which obviously wasn't going to help her now. She counted what usable money she had, then tentatively laid out the amount that the desk clerk had entered on the printed card. If she was very, very careful, she might last two or three days before she ran out of cash.

Mattie stared at the bills Kiera had so carefully and reluctantly counted out, then looked up again. Kiera shifted uncomfortably when the other woman studied her face.

"Husband or boyfriend?"

"Excuse me?"

"Honey, I know it ain't none of my beeswax," Mattie stated flatly. "But it's hard not to notice that shiner you got there."

Instinctively, Kiera reached up and pulled her hair forward. *So much for makeup.* "No—I— It's not like that. I fell off a horse."

Sympathy softened the harsh edges of Mattie's eyes. "Like I said, it's none of my beeswax. But a woman comes into my motel late at night, alone, looking like she's been chewed up and spit out, and I can't help it, it's my Christian duty to ask."

Do I really look that bad? Kiera thought, biting her lip. She glanced down at her rumpled clothes, knew her eyes were probably still red from crying, and she realized that she *did* look that bad.

"If you need an ear or a shoulder…" Mattie went on "…I know a few things about men. I hear there's a few good ones around, but, honey, my experience is most of them are asses."

At the moment, Kiera might tend to agree with that assessment but decided against encouraging the topic. "If I could just get my key."

"Sure." Mattie shrugged a shoulder, dropped the money into a drawer, then held out a key. "Room 107."

"Thanks."

"You know," the desk clerk said when Kiera turned. "If you decide to stick around for a while and need a job, they're hiring at the hotel in town."

"Thank you, but—"

"I could put a good word in for you," Mattie offered. "My sister, Janet, is head of human resources. I'm sure she could find a spot for you."

"I'm really not—"

"You don't even have to have any experience," Mattie continued. "They got all kinds of jobs open since they expanded. Between conventions and conferences and the new wedding chapel, the place is packed most of the time. I hear the new owner, Clair Blackhawk is great to work for."

Blackhawk?

The name sucked the breath out of Kiera's lungs. She stared at the desk clerk, had to swallow before she managed a weak reply. "Blackhawk?"

"Well, that *was* her name, but she got married a few weeks ago, so I'm not sure what her last name is now. Oh, wait—" Mattie snapped her fingers "—it's Carver. Clair Carver."

With her heart clamoring so loudly, it was hard for

Kiera to concentrate. The name Carver meant nothing to her. But Blackhawk… *God, was it possible?* It was all she could do not to grab the desk clerk's arm, ask her point-blank if—"

"You okay, honey?"

Kiera blinked, watched Mattie's face come back into focus. "What?"

"You look a little pale. You feelin' okay?"

"It's just been a long day." *The longest of my life,* she thought, and forced a smile. "I appreciate your concern, but, really, I'll be fine."

Mattie nodded. "You're the last room on the left, just past the ice and vending machines. You need anything, just give me a call."

"Thanks."

Knees shaking, Kiera turned and walked back to her car. She wasn't certain how long she sat there, dazed, staring blankly into the deep shadows of the poplars edging the motel. As a child, she'd always been afraid of the dark, knew that ferocious monsters lived there, waiting to swallow children whole.

At twenty-five, maybe she was still a little afraid of the dark, she realized.

When she walked back into the motel office, Mattie glanced up from the TV.

Kiera closed the door behind her. "About that job…"

When Sam Prescott made his morning rounds through the lobby of the Four Winds Hotel, bellmen straightened their shoulders, desk clerks smiled brighter, valets hustled. The entire staff of Wolf River County's largest and most luxurious hotel knew that nothing slipped past the general manager's penetrating gaze. The white marble floors and vast expanse of glass windows had better sparkle, the chic black uniforms be crisp, the massive floral arrangements fresh.

The sharp, sculpted planes of Sam's face and the hard angle of his jaw played well with his thick, dark hair and deep brown eyes. It was a combination that made grown women sigh and young girls giggle. Even with his football player's chest and lean waist, Sam's six-foot-four inch frame wore Armani well.

A few lucky women knew he wore nothing at all even better.

Joseph McFearson, the Four Winds doorman, tipped his hat when Sam approached. "Mornin', Mr. Prescott."

"Mornin', Joseph." Joseph was one of the few employees whose height—and eyes—directly met Sam's. "How's Isabel?"

"On a rampage our boys don't call more often," Joseph groused. "Says they got their father's cold heart."

Sam grinned. Everyone knew Joseph had a heart of gold, just as everyone knew that his wife adored him. "Give her my best."

"Will do." Joseph nodded, then added when Sam walked by, "Call your mother."

I probably should, Sam thought, realizing he hadn't talked to her for a while. Maybe he'd just send flowers. Last time he'd called her, all he'd heard was, "Samuel, you're thirty-two years old, when are you going to stop living in hotels and give me more grandchildren?"

"Soon as I meet a girl like you," he'd say to placate

way....

"Six?" *Turn,* he thought. *Just a couple of in*

She didn't. "Yes, thank you."

There was no smile in her voice. M

handle-it-don't-bother-me polite to

Discreetly, he watched her i

after all, he reasoned, part of h

in his hotel. She seemed te

just a little too straight,

tight. The sixth floor

meant she was her

He started to

in his jacket p

at the call

The

hurri

th

stepped inside, her head

through a white purse.

She was taller than average, maybe five-nine, slender. Shoulder-length hair, shiny as polished coal, swept softly across her shoulders. Her suit was pale pink, the lace-edged camisole under the jacket lime-green. She'd turned away so he couldn't see her face.

Damn, she smelled good.

"What floor?" he offered, lifting a hand to the button panel.

"I've got it."

She started to punch a button on her side of the elevator, then pulled away when she saw it was already lit.

ches this

...lore of an I-can-
...ne.

...n the mirror—it was,
...s job to notice the people
...nse. Her shoulders and back
...he grip on her purse a little too
...was all offices, which probably
...e for business of some sort.

...introduce himself when the cell phone
...ocket buzzed. He pulled it out and glanced
...r ID. Clair.

...levator doors opened smoothly and the woman
...d away. Sam stepped out, watched her walk down
...e hall, enjoyed the gentle sway of feminine hips and
purposeful stride of long, sexy legs. When she paused
at the door to Human Resources, he sighed. Too bad. If
she was here for a job, his fantasy of soft black hair
sliding over his naked chest was shattered.

Rule Number One: He did not date employees.

When his phone vibrated again, he flipped it open.
"Mornin', Boss."

"You can be boss today, Prescott. In fact, I think I'll
just give you the Four Winds and crawl back to my bed."

Sam frowned. "What's wrong?"

"I think the bug my nephews had last week decided
to visit me, too," she said weakly. "Will you ask Suz to
reschedule my appointments?"

"Sure." He noticed the woman was still standing

outside Human Resources, though it seemed a bit odd she had put her hand on the doorknob and not moved. "You need soup or something sent over?"

"Please," she groaned, "don't mention food. And Jacob's home today, so if I—oh, God, not again. Bye."

The line clicked dead. *Poor kid,* Sam sympathized, slipping his phone back into his pocket. He could think of much better ways to spend a day in bed.

That thought drew his glance back down the hall. The woman was gone. He could still smell her, though. A soft, pretty fragrance that seemed to whisper in his ear.

Damn.

He'd never even seen her face.

Heaving a sigh, he glanced at his watch and headed for his office, hesitated briefly outside of Human Resources, then kept going. Since Clair had cancelled their morning meeting, this would be a good time to get a jump on the end-of-the-month reports. At the rate the Four Winds was growing, he could barely keep up with the paperwork. He didn't have time to traipse after beautiful, mysterious women.

Halfway down the hall, he stopped.

Oh, hell, why not?

Even if she was applying for a job, she wasn't an employee *yet,* he figured. He turned back around and headed back for Human Resources. He might as well satisfy his curiosity while he had the chance. No harm in putting a face to that sexy body.

He stepped into the office and glanced around. Janet's secretary was not at her desk, and the door to the inner office was closed. The waiting room was empty.

Damn. He'd already missed her.

Slipping his hands into his pockets, Sam wandered closer to the closed door.

"I see you've had some restaurant experience, Miss Daniels," Sam heard Janet say. "Anything in particular?"

"Hostess, waitress, bussing," the woman replied. "Some kitchen training."

"Are you available nights, weekends and on call?"

Sam waited for the woman to mention a husband or children, but she didn't, simply answered that she was available whenever she was needed.

"Miss Daniels—"

"Please, call me Kiera."

"Kiera, you haven't listed any references on your application. Could you give me your last place of employment?"

"No, Mrs. Lamott. I—I'm sorry, but I can't."

No references? Sam lowered his brow. Janet couldn't possibly hire the woman without references.

"Kiera." Janet's voice softened. "My sister explained your situation to me, which is why I'm meeting with you so quickly."

Situation? Sam leaned closer to the door. What situation?

"I appreciate it, and I assure you, I'm a hard worker and learn quickly." Desperation edged the woman's voice. "I'll work any hours you ask, do whatever you need me to do, but please just give me a chance."

Sam narrowed his eyes and frowned. He didn't care what the woman looked like, or what her "situation"

was. The Four Winds was not a charity. It was a
business. They hired people based on qualifications,
not because they said *please*.

Rule Number Two: Hotel policies applied equally to
the *entire* staff.

Sam wished like hell he could see what was going
on inside the office. He could hear both women
speaking, but they'd lowered their voices and he
couldn't make out their words. His ear was all but
touching the door when he heard Janet speak again.

"Can you start tomorrow?"

What? Sam raised his head, then stared at the door
and frowned. Janet had actually hired this woman
without any references at all?

"Yes, of course I can start tomorrow. Thank you."
The woman's voice trembled. "Thank you so much.
You won't be sorry, I promise you."

"Go downstairs to the lower lobby employee entrance
and ask for Francine. She'll fit you for a uniform."

He rarely interfered with the head of a department,
but there were times it was necessary. Anything that
took place here at the Four Winds was ultimately his re-
sponsibility, and that included hiring and firing. He
straightened, set his jaw and prepared himself to face
both women. Janet might not like it, but if he had to
supersede a decision, then she'd just have to—

The door opened, and his mind simply went blank.

Her face was everything he'd imagined and quite
a bit more. A sensuous, delicate sculpture of high
cheekbones, straight nose and wide, full mouth.
Smooth, sun-bronzed skin against deep, smoky-blue

eyes. Eyes that considerably widened when they met his.

The faint tinge of black and blue next to one of those bewitching eyes was like a sucker punch in his gut.

"Sam, I didn't know you were here." Smiling, Janet moved to the door. "This is Kiera Daniels. Kiera, Sam Prescott, general manager of the Four Winds."

"Mr. Prescott." Kiera's smile never made her eyes. "How do you do."

He took the hand she offered; it was as soft as it was warm. "We're not formal here, Kiera. Just Sam."

"I hired Kiera for the lunch shift at Adagio's," Janet said. "She's on her way downstairs to see Francine."

"Welcome to the Four Winds." He realized he was still holding the woman's hand and reluctantly let go. "I'm headed in that direction. Why don't I show you the way?"

"I wouldn't want to trouble you." Kiera hitched her purse a little higher on her shoulder. "I can find my way."

"I'm sure you can." He kept his gaze steady with hers. "But it's no trouble at all."

He saw the resistance in her eyes, knew she wanted to refuse his offer but, under the circumstances, couldn't. He'd cornered her, and she countered with a lift of her chin and a nod.

Janet looked at Sam. "Was there something you needed?"

Something he needed? Oh, right. He *had* been lurking outside her office, hadn't he? "I want to take some stats into my lunch meeting with the Cattlemen's Association. I'd like to reassure them we have the staff to handle a convention their size."

"No problem." Janet's gaze shifted to Kiera and softened. "If you have any questions, or if you need anything at all, please don't hesitate to call me."

Sam set his back teeth. Obviously, Janet had let her heart rule her decision, not her head.

Rule Number Three: Do not get emotionally attached.

Which he wouldn't. But what he *would* do, at least for the moment, was trust Janet's decision.

And keep an eye on Miss Kiera Daniels himself.

"I know how busy you must be," Kiera said politely when he walked with her in the hallway. "I hate to trouble you."

"No trouble." He pressed the elevator button, slipped his hands casually into his pants' pockets. "My ten o'clock meeting was cancelled."

Her lips pressed into a tight smile before she turned away to adjust the strap of her purse. With her attention elsewhere, he allowed himself the pleasure of drawing her scent into his lungs, held it there for a long moment.

And for reasons that had nothing to do with hotel policy, wished like hell Janet *hadn't* hired her.

"In fact—" he followed her onto the elevator when the doors slid open, made a decision he was certain he'd regret "—since I'm free for the next hour, why don't I give you a tour?"

Two

Kiera was certain she hadn't heard him right. She cleared her throat and calmly met his eyes. Dark, intense eyes, that seemed to bore straight through her. "A tour?"

"Every person on the staff needs to know their way around the hotel." He pushed the elevator button. "But if you haven't the time…"

"Not at all." Why would he do this? She'd worked in hotels before, knew perfectly well that the general manager didn't take new employees on a tour. She also knew perfectly well she couldn't refuse. "Now is fine."

"Good."

The smile he gave her made her pulse jump. Something told her that very few people—especially women—ever said no to Sam Prescott. He had a…*presence,* she thought. Not just his height, or the broad stretch of shoulders. Not even those lethal eyes, strong jaw and thick, espresso-brown hair.

No, it was much more than the way he looked. The first time she'd stepped into the elevator with him, she'd *felt* it.

Power.

The air inside the elevator had sizzled with it. She'd intentionally kept her gaze turned from him, even when she'd felt the gripping pull to look. Perhaps for self-preservation, perhaps to prove to herself that she *could* resist. She hadn't even been able to breathe until she'd stepped out of the elevator.

And here she was again. Same elevator. Same man. Same sizzle.

Trey had told her on more than one occasion that she was naive. When they'd argued before she'd left the ranch, he'd told her again. So maybe she was. But she wasn't *so* naive to think that Sam Prescott standing outside Mrs. Lamott's office door was an accident. And she wasn't so naive to think that this *tour* he wanted to take her on was hotel policy.

She certainly hadn't done anything to attract this man's unwanted attention. As far as he knew, she was simply a new employee—a waitress. There was nothing about her that should warrant interest from a general manager.

Unless he suspected she wasn't being completely honest…

Oh, good grief, Kiera, she silently chided herself. *You're being paranoid.* Of *course* he doesn't suspect anything. How could he?

This has to be the slowest elevator I've ever been on.

"You're not from around here," he said flatly.

She hesitated, decided that the best way to avoid questions was to offer information. It might be useless information, but she hoped it would alleviate any apprehensions he might have about her. "I was born and raised in East Texas. Have you heard of a town called Rainville?"

"Can't say that I have."

"It's not exactly a tourist spot." It wasn't *exactly* where she was from, either, though it was close. "Unless you're interested in honey."

"Honey?"

"Rainville's claim to fame." When the elevator finally slid to a stop, she stepped forward. "They raise bees."

"Really."

When he pressed the button to keep the doors closed, then leveled those piercing eyes at her, Kiera's stomach twisted.

"What happened to your eye?" he asked.

Her eye? Confused, she stared at him. Oh, her *eye*. She'd forgotten about that. She released the breath she'd been holding, waited a moment for her pulse to slow down. "I fell off a horse."

His frown darkened. "I'm not asking to be nosy. If you have a problem that might become this hotel's problem, I need to know."

So *that's* what he was suspicious about, she realized. Not because he knew who she was or that she lied but because of her black eye. Relief poured through her. "Everyone has problems, Mr. Prescott," she said evenly. "But I assure you, whatever mine are, they will in no way affect my job or this hotel."

He stared at her for a long, nerve-racking moment,

then removed his finger from the button. "Sam," he said and straightened.

The elevator doors opened and he stepped out.

On unsteady legs, she followed.

The decor at Adagio's Ristorante was elegant and contemporary. Crisp white linens, airy palms and high ceilings invited diners to relax, while the menu invited them to indulge. Homemade fusilli, a carpaccio sauce that made even the most hardened critic shed tears and "the best crème brûlée on the northern continent," according to one reviewer, had made the restaurant legendary in the few short years it had been open.

The fragrant scent of warm spices and fresh bread mixed with the clink of tableware. The lunch crowd was always louder than dinner, and the animated voices of hotel guests and local business owners filled the softly lit room.

Sitting in a corner booth, Sam speared a bite of the steak he'd ordered, chewed attentively while Rachel Forster, publicist for the Central Texas Cattlemen's Association, discussed her schedule.

"I'll be sending out a press release to all the local newspapers within a hundred-mile radius, and I have a photographer coming out next Tuesday," Rachel said. "I'll have him call to set up an appointment."

It was more information than Sam really needed, but the blonde sitting across from him, young, extremely efficient and heavily armed with pages of notes, seemed determined to go over every minute detail of the upcoming conference.

"I'd also like to write an article for *The Dallas Register* on the Four Winds chef. I understand he's won the Hotelier's Choice Award three years in a row. I thought maybe I could tie that in with some kind of a Texas beef angle."

"Chef Bartollini is on hiatus for the next six months." Actually, he'd flown home to Italy for a family emergency, and, unfortunately, no one knew when, or if, the man would return. "Chef Phillipe Girard is with us until then."

"Would it be possible for me to meet him?" she asked.

Not a good idea, Sam thought, but simply smiled. "I'll see what I can do."

"I'd appreciate that, and oh, I was wondering—" she pushed her black-rimmed glasses up the bridge of her nose and scribbled on her notepad "—I'd like to meet the new owner and get some background so I can write a story about her, as well."

"She's out of the office today." Sam doubted that Clair would consent to an interview. Even though most of the people in Wolf River knew her family history, Clair wouldn't want it printed in newspapers across the state. "Why don't I have her secretary call you?"

When the publicist moved on to the next item on her list, transportation issues, Sam listened patiently. Well, *half* listened, anyway.

He glanced across the crowded restaurant to the serving station, where Kiera busily filled water glasses with ice. Francine had already fitted her with Adagio's standard uniform: white, long-sleeved shirt and tailored black slacks. The only variation the restaurant allowed for the servers was their personal choice of tie. Kiera's was silver, with thin stripes of white and black. She'd knotted her dark hair on top of her head and secured it with shiny red chopsticks. The style not only revealed her long, slender neck but gave her an exotic look, as well.

Unwanted, restless, something stirred in him.

The tour he'd taken her on had included the lobby, conference rooms, employee gym and wedding chapel. She'd paid attention and asked several questions regarding hotel policies but had kept a stiff, polite demeanor. In itself, that wasn't odd, he reasoned. New employees were usually nervous around him. But with Kiera, she hadn't seemed nervous as much as simply reluctant to be anywhere near him.

Especially when he'd questioned her about her eye.

I fell off a horse.

Who the hell did she think she was kidding with that line? She might as well have said she'd walked into a doorknob, for God's sake. And why the hell should he believe her problems wouldn't follow her here? Because she'd said so?

She was hiding something, that much was obvious. For now, he decided he'd simply keep an eye on her.

Which was exactly what he was doing, he thought, watching as she hefted the tray of water glasses. When she moved smoothly toward a table of noisy businessmen, the silver in her tie shimmered.

Dammit. Why the hell did he think that tie looked so damn sexy?

"Will that be possible?"

Sam realized the publicist had asked him a question,

something about the banquet meals, and he snapped his attention back to her. He had no idea what the woman had said, so he flashed a smile. "I'll personally work with the catering department to see that your every need is met."

"Oh—" Flustered, Rachel's face turned rose-pink. She fumbled through her papers. "Well, thank you. Ah, now if we could go over the local publicity I've planned, I'd like to be sure it meets with your approval."

"Of course." With a silent sigh, Sam dragged his mind off the woman serving water several feet away and back to his job.

"Hey, babe, I need two iced teas and one soda at table six, one coffee, one soda at eight, refills at ten and eleven."

Kiera quickly memorized and filled the order, didn't bother to take the time to be annoyed that Tyler, the server she'd been paired with her first day, had pretty much called her everything except her name. She understood there was a pecking order in every restaurant, and as the new girl she was going to have to take her share of hits. She'd been there before and she could handle it.

What she couldn't handle, she thought, hefting the tray of drinks, was Sam Prescott.

He'd been watching her from that corner booth for the past hour. He hadn't been obvious about it, but, nonetheless, she'd been very aware that he'd been keeping track of her. As if it wasn't difficult enough that this was her first day on the job and she had to not only learn the staff's names, the layout of the restaurant and the stations, but keep her orders straight so Tyler-honey-baby-sugar-darling wouldn't be on her back.

While she smiled and dropped off the first order of two iced teas and a soda, she casually glanced in Sam's direction. He sat with a cupid-faced blonde who wore thick-framed glasses and a tailored pantsuit the color of buttered toast. They appeared to be having a serious conversation, although the woman was doing most of the talking, while Sam simply listened and nodded.

She knew he didn't trust her, and that tour he'd taken her on had been more of a fishing expedition than anything else. Even his questions hadn't been all that subtle.

Have you been in town long? Not really.

Will your husband be joining you? No.

So what brings you to Wolf River?

She'd wanted to say, "A car," but managed a response that was much more vague and certainly more polite. Her answers hadn't satisfied him, but something told her that Sam Prescott was not a man who was easily satisfied.

She knew all about men like that.

His gaze suddenly lifted and met hers. The knot of stress in her stomach twisted a little tighter, but she managed to curve her lips into what she hoped looked like a smile, then moved on and finished delivering her drinks. She hadn't even dropped off the tray in her hands before Tyler thrust another one at her.

"Take these salads to table ten. One chicken barbecue and one Caesar. And hurry it up, will you, toots? Table six is waiting for more bread."

Toots? Kiera ground her teeth, bit the inside of her lip, then turned with the tray.

And froze.

Trey?

Kiera stared at the man talking to the hostess. His back was turned to her, but it *had* to be Trey. Same wavy devil-black hair, same broad shoulders, same bronzed skin. That all-too familiar stance of arrogant authority.

Oh, God. She felt the blood drain from her face. *How had he found her?*

"Move it, sweet cheeks."

Startled at the sudden voice behind her, Kiera swung around too quickly and knocked the tray into Tyler. To her horror—and Tyler's—the food went down the front of him. The tray and salad plates crashed to the ground.

"You *idiot!*" Tyler hissed under his breath while he swiped at the bits of shredded lettuce and diced tomatoes clinging to his white shirt and burgundy tie. Barbecue sauce dripped from his collar.

Every head in the restaurant turned her way, but Kiera only cared about one. She glanced back toward the hostess desk, locked her gaze with a pair of curious dark brown eyes.

Oh, thank God.

It *wasn't* Trey.

Even as Tyler continued to berate her, overwhelming relief swam through her. Relief that quickly dissipated when Chef Phillipe Girard stepped through the double kitchen doors.

Her first thought was he looked like a rutabaga, round at the top, narrow at the bottom. Fleshy cheeks framed an oversized nose and underscored pale, deep-set eyes. A tall, black chef's hat sat like an exclamation point on top of a sand-colored ponytail. He had a knife in one hand and an onion in the other.

Kiera had heard about the man from a couple of the other servers. She'd been warned, "Stay out of his way," "Don't make him mad" and double-warned, "Don't mess with his food."

In the span of less than thirty seconds, she'd managed to do all three.

Based on the chef's ominous frown, Kiera had the feeling he'd like to dice and chop more than onions. He glared down his large nose at her.

"Clean this mess up immediately," he snarled, then he turned and swept back into the kitchen.

Releasing the breath she'd been holding, Kiera bent and picked up the tray and broken salad plates.

"You've done it now, miss butterfingers," Tyler hissed, still brushing bits of green and red from his shirt. "He'll take it out on all of us and God only knows what hell he'll put—"

"Tyler, that's enough."

Kiera looked up and met Sam's somber gaze. She couldn't quite read his expression, but when he shifted his attention to Tyler, Sam's mouth hardened.

"It wasn't my fault." Tyler pursed his lips. "I was just—"

"Never mind. Go change your shirt. Christine can cover for you until you get back."

"Yes, sir." Tyler tossed a look of annoyance at Kiera as he flounced off.

A busboy appeared with a trash bag and hand broom. When Sam cupped a hand on her elbow, Kiera pulled away. "I'll finish here," she said anxiously, still picking up chunks of broken plate. "I can help with those tables, too."

"Not necessary." Sam wrapped his fingers around her arm, tighter this time, and pulled her up. "Come with me."

Every bone in her body, every *cell,* vibrated in protest. *Terrific.* Just what she needed. One more lecture. He released her arm and turned away. Because she didn't want to make a scene—again—she followed Sam through the restaurant, down a hallway of offices, then outside to a shaded back alley.

An air conditioning motor whirred and blew hot air over her feet; in the distance, church bells chimed the three o'clock hour.

She lifted her chin, prepared herself to be fired. *A perfect end to the perfect day.*

"What happened in there?" he asked.

"I tripped."

He frowned at her. "Has anyone ever told you that you're a lousy liar?"

Trey, she thought. And Alexis and Alaina. But she sure as hell didn't need *this* man telling her. Still, common sense overrode defiance, and rather than speak she pressed her lips firmly together and stared blankly at him.

"You didn't trip, Kiera," he said evenly. "I was watching you. Something spooked you."

"Maybe it was you watching me."

He lifted an eyebrow. "Do I make you nervous?"

"It's not unusual to be nervous when the boss is staring at you."

"You have an interesting way of avoiding a direct answer to a direct question." He studied her face. "Do *I* make *you* nervous?"

Yes, dammit, she thought. But she had no intention

of admitting it. She glanced over her shoulder. "I really should be getting back to work."

"You turned white as your blouse when you looked at Rand," Sam replied, ignoring her comment. "Do you know him?"

"Rand?" she asked calmly, but her heart skipped a beat. Sam had obviously seen her staring at the man who looked so much like Trey. "Who is Rand?"

"There you go again." Sighing, he shook his head. "Rand Blackhawk. He moved back to Wolf River a few months ago, got married. He's rebuilding the family ranch outside of town."

She gave him her best I'm-really-not-interested expression, but her heart was beating fast. "Fascinating story, but I've never seen him before."

Sam moved closer. "But he looks like someone you know, doesn't he? Someone you're worried might find you."

He was too close, not only in his estimation of her situation, but physically. Close enough she could see the subtle but fierce striations of deep brown in his irises, the web of lines at the corners of his eyes, the thick fringe of lashes. His scent was pure male, and the female in her reluctantly responded.

"No one is looking for me, Mr. Prescott." For once, she could answer a question truthfully. At least, she *prayed* it was true. "Now if you're going to fire me, then fire me. Otherwise, I'd appreciate it if you'd let me get back to work."

He stared at her for a long moment, then stepped back. "I'll speak to the chef. I know he can be difficult."

She knew that Chef Phillipe would only dislike her all the more if Sam said even one word to him about her. "Thank you, but that's really not necessary."

Somehow she managed to walk away without stumbling or without looking back. In the employee restroom, she let out a long breath, shook off her jitters, then washed her hands and returned to her station. The spill had been cleaned up and Tyler had changed into a clean shirt and tie. His surly attitude, however, remained the same. He glared at her and gestured to a pitcher of iced tea.

"Refills at ten and twelve, miss grace, if you think you can manage without spilling anything."

Enough was enough.

Narrowing her eyes, Kiera moved in close to the server, stuck her face nose to nose with his and pressed a fingertip against his bony chest. "My name is Kiera. Got that? *Kiera.* Next time you call me anything else, next time you insult me, next time you even look at me with disrespect, you're going to be wearing more than a few scraps of lettuce and barbecue sauce."

Smiling, she smoothed a hand over the startled server's clean tie, then turned and picked up the iced tea. Red-faced, Tyler moved out of her way.

So much for keeping things low key, she thought while she refilled glasses. Rand Blackhawk. She glanced at the man now sitting in a booth with a pretty redhead, then quickly looked away before she did something stupid.

Too late, she thought with a sigh, then watched Sam walk back into the restaurant.

Way too late.

Three

With the Fourth of July only two weeks away, the town of Wolf River had already tuned up to celebrate. Red-white-and-blue bunting adorned the two-story brick store-fronts down Main Street, patriotic slogans welcomed tourists, posters announced an upcoming rodeo and carnival. The holiday would bring in tourists from across the country and locals as far away as Houston.

It might be a small town, but it was a busy small town.

And growing every day, Sam noted as he strolled down the sidewalk. On Main Street, the city council had carefully kept Wolf River's country charm through strict building ordinances, but off the main drag they had slowly allowed the big city in. Three-story office buildings, two fast-food restaurants, a small water park, a multiplex theater and the most recent addition, a country-western dinner house with live entertainment and nightly line dancing. Sam had heard the rib-eye steaks were as thick as a phone book and tender as warm butter. He made a mental note to check it out for himself soon.

"Gonna be a hot one," Fergus Crum said dryly. The old man had been pushing a broom across the sidewalk in front of the hardware store, but he stopped and rested his arthritic hands on the broom handle when he spotted Sam coming his way.

"Come by the bar after work," Sam said as he passed. "Have a cold one on me."

"I'll do that." Fergus was never one to turn down a cold beer. Or any beer, for that matter. "How 'bout some of those onion thingies, too?"

"You got it."

Sam nodded at a local rancher coming out of the barbershop and the man touched the brim of his cowboy hat. Even though Sam knew most of the locals, he didn't come into town very often. He had no reason to. Most everything he needed he could get at the hotel. Food, clothes, even a car. He had few personal possessions, considered them a hindrance when it was time to pick up and move on. He kept his life—professional and personal—simple.

Exactly how he liked it.

His two-year contract with the Four Winds had been up for two months now. Clair had been pressing him to sign a new one, but he'd put her off. He figured it was about time to start putting out feelers for his next job. His entire life, he'd never lived more than three years in one place. He had no intention of breaking that record any time soon.

"Hey, handsome, where you headed?"

Sam smiled when Olivia Cameron pulled her sleek red Camaro up to the curb alongside him. The stunning redhead owned Vintage Rose, one of the antique stores in Wolf River and she'd also done the interior design on the lobby in the Four Winds.

He leaned into her open car window and gave her a kiss on the cheek. "On my way to the courthouse, gorgeous."

Her green eyes sparkled. "You finally going to apply for our marriage license?"

"Just say the word, Liv." They'd gone out on a couple of dates, but the chemistry hadn't quite been there between them, so they'd settled into a more comfortable, flirtatious friendship. "We could buy one of those tract homes they're building in Oak Meadows. Have a half dozen kids and join the PTA."

Olivia winced. "I'll get back to you one of these decades. Want a ride?"

He straightened and patted his stomach. "Walk will do me good."

"As if you need it. Every woman in this town knows you work out from five to six-thirty every morning in the Four Winds gym." Olivia gunned her engine. "Why do you think there are so many females in there at that ungodly hour?"

With a wink, Olivia shot away from the curb.

Grinning, Sam watched her disappear around the corner, wished there had been chemistry between them. Like him, the woman wasn't looking for a commitment or a picket fence. They could have simply enjoyed each other, without worrying about the theatrics or complications of a messy breakup. Olivia could have been an enjoyable distraction.

And Lord knew, right now he certainly needed one.

He'd spent the past three days watching Kiera. Watched her effortlessly memorize the menu and wine list. Watched her skillfully serve a heavy tray of dishes without fumbling or getting an order wrong. Watched her astutely make recommendations, then offer suggestions for a complimentary wine. Already, she not only had people asking for her station but actually waiting for her.

He'd never seen anything like it.

But—to his annoyance—he hadn't just been watching her. He'd also been *thinking* about her.

At the most unexpected times, he'd suddenly find himself wondering what the woman's story was, who or what she was running away from. If she was in some kind of danger.

The bruise next to her eye had nearly disappeared, but he couldn't get the image out of his mind. Couldn't stop the raw fury that knotted his gut every time he thought about it. The idea of some man raising his fist and—

Realizing he had balled his own hand into a tight fist, he stopped in front of the barbershop, stared at the swirling red-white-and-blue pole. He loosened his fingers, then shook off the anger bubbling through his blood. Dammit! A walk through town on his day off should have cleared his mind and relaxed him, and here he was, barreling down the sidewalk as if he were looking for a fight.

Maybe I am, he thought with a sigh. Lord knew the woman had frustrated him enough. It was obvious she had a problem, obvious that she'd been scared to death when she'd looked at Rand Blackhawk. Obvious she was lying about something. When he'd asked her if Rand looked like someone she knew, the answer in those smoky blue eyes of hers had obviously been *yes.*

And *obviously,* she hadn't wanted his help.

So fine. Why should that bother him?

He waited for a truck to pass, then crossed the street leading to the courthouse. As long as her problem didn't become the hotel's, then he'd keep his nose out of her mess. Lord knew he'd already given Kiera Daniels way too much time and thought. He was a busy man. With the upcoming conferences and events, not to mention the impending construction on the hotel, his focus needed to be on his job, not a pretty waitress.

And then suddenly that pretty waitress was walking out of the glass courthouse doors.

Surprised, he stopped beside a hedge of white blooming roses. Good God, he thought with annoyance. He couldn't even get away from her here.

Head bent, loose-limbed, she moved down the courthouse steps, her eyes focused on a piece of paper in her hand. She wore denim as if it had been invented just for those endlessly long legs of hers. Her jeans, low on her hips and snug, were faded in all the places a man liked to look. And touch. Her white tank top dipped demurely across her collarbone and hugged her breasts, then rose just high enough from her hips to show the barest hint of smooth, flat stomach.

A drought settled in his throat.

It took a will of iron to drag his gaze upward from that enticing glimpse of skin. A frown drew the delicate line of her eyebrows together and settled into a somber line across her mouth. Her hair flowed like a black river down her shoulders. The sun glinted off the dark strands.

For a split second, he didn't even know where he was.

He blinked hard, watched her fold the piece of paper and shove it into a black tote bag as she turned and walked in the opposite direction.

He argued with himself, lost, waited a full twenty seconds, then followed her.

The mouth-watering scent of grilling hamburgers drew Kiera toward the coffee shop on the corner. The exterior of the restaurant, shiny chrome, sleek lines and wrap-around windows reminded her of the '57 Chevy that Mr. Mackelroy, her high school principal, used to drive. Even the color was the same, she thought. Sorbet-blue.

When she stepped inside, life-size cardboard cut-outs of James Dean and Marilyn Monroe greeted her with a sign that said Welcome To Pappa Pete's. Kiera closed the door behind her, barely heard the jangling of the bells over the drumming of a Beach Boys song playing on an overhead speaker and the lively conversations from the lunch crowd. Locals, Kiera thought, noting the mix of families, town workers and ranch hands.

A tall, thick-boned, platinum blonde carrying four plates of burgers on one arm and two plates of French fries on the other bustled by Kiera. "Set yerself down anywhere you like, honey. Something to drink?"

Kiera smiled. "Lemonade, please."

"Hey, Madge, what about me?" A slumped-back cowboy sitting at a counter stool held up his coffee cup. "I'm still waiting for a refill."

"You're still waitin' for brains, too," Madge shot back. "Everyone knows you were in the basement when they got handed out."

"Yeah, well, everyone knows you were at the front door when tongues got handed out," the cowboy quipped, which brought a round of laughter from the patrons.

"Least I got something in my skull that works." Madge plunked the fries down on a table. "If your thinker was a mattress, an ant's feet would stick off the sides."

"That's not all I heard was ant size," someone in the front hollered, setting off a fresh round of laughter and a volley of replies. Red-faced, the cowboy got up, snatched a coffeepot from behind the counter and served himself.

While the wisecracks continued to fly, Kiera sat down at a Formica-topped table next to a window in the back. A teenage boy who hadn't quite grown into his long legs and arms set a glass of pink lemonade in front of her. She smiled and thanked the busboy, who turned beet-red, then turned and stumbled over his own big feet. One of the ranchers teased the boy, which set in motion a new volley of quips.

If she closed her eyes, she could almost imagine she was in her own hometown, sitting in the Bronco Cafe, adding her own two cents to the banter and good-natured fun. Even the smell was the same. Burgers, grease and pressed wood paneling. A good smell, she thought. Familiar. Comfortable. Since graduating college, then working her fanny off at restaurants across the country, she could probably count on one hand the times she'd even been back to the Bronco in the past six years.

Living in a small town could be difficult, she knew. The gossip, the politics, certainly the lack of privacy, all of it was a major pain in the butt. The closest city with a mall had been three hours away, the only theater showed movies two months old and the few dates she had been on had felt more like going out with a best friend or a brother.

But the camaraderie, knowing that there were always people who would pull together and help if you needed them, people who really gave a damn, was worth not only the isolation she'd often felt at Stone Ridge Ranch, but the aggravation of everyone knowing her family's business.

And now the question was, *did* everyone know?

She certainly hadn't.

With a sigh, she pulled the piece of paper out of her bag and spread it on the table in front of her, stared at the obituary, felt every word etch into her brain like acid.

William Blackhawk…local rancher, business-man and community leader…died in a small plane crash…survived by his son, Dillon Black-hawk…services to be held Thursday at Wolf River Community Church…

That was two years ago.

Two years.

She closed her eyes against the fresh wave of pain coursing through her. If she'd known then what she knew now, what would she have done?

She honestly didn't know.

"Mind if I join you?"

Jolted out of her thoughts by the question, the terse "yes" on the edge of her tongue nearly slipped out. Her pulse jumped when she looked up.

Sam.

She prayed her hands weren't visibly shaking as she folded the piece of paper and slipped it back into her bag. Despite the fact that she would have preferred to be alone at the moment, she couldn't very well tell her boss to take a hike.

And since he had already slid into the booth across from her, he really hadn't given her much of a choice, anyway.

When she glanced around the room, several curious eyes quickly looked away. Terrific. No one in the diner knew who she was, but everyone in the place surely knew who Sam Prescott was. Before the day was over, Kiera had no doubt that rumors of the Four Winds general manager having an afternoon rendezvous with an unknown woman would be burning up the phone lines.

Sam followed her gaze. "You expecting someone?"

"No." She looked back at him, took in the street clothes he wore. She'd thought him handsome in a suit. Confident. Absolutely unwavering and completely sure of himself. But it had nothing to do with clothes, she realized, taking in the stretch of black T-shirt across his broad shoulders and muscled arms. Apparently, the rumors she'd heard about him working out in the gym every morning were true. "I was just running errands and stopped in for something to eat."

"You picked the right place." He leaned in close and whispered, "Best hamburger in town, though if you tell anyone I said so, I'll deny it."

The smile on his mouth disarmed her, had her whispering back, "I think I can manage to keep a secret."

"Yeah." He studied her for a moment. "I think you can."

She stilled at his comment, arched an eyebrow and settled back in her chair. "You sure you aren't here for fish, Mr. Prescott?"

Smiling, he settled back in his chair, as well.

An unseen cook in the kitchen dinged three times on a bell to signal an order was up.

Round one, Kiera thought absently.

"So how's it going?" Sam asked.

"I assume you're referring to my job."

"Of course."

She picked up her lemonade, sipped. "Why don't you tell me?"

"Okay." He folded his hands on the table and straightened his shoulders. "Your ratio of tables to gross and time are in the ninetieth percentile and an initial review of customer comments is exceptional."

In spite of the deep, official tone of his voice, Kiera saw the glint of a rogue in Sam's eyes. "Sounds like I should ask for a raise."

"I'm afraid that request would be denied. You've had two complaints filed against you."

"What!" Lemonade sloshed over the rim of her glass and ran down the front of her tank top; a sliver of ice slid under the cotton neckline and into her bra. Frowning, she grabbed a napkin.

He signaled for the busboy. "Tyler says you're difficult to work with."

Tyler's an ass, she nearly said, but managed to bite her tongue. She'd worked with jerks like him before. He was a good waiter, but he kissed up to the manager and chef, patronized the rest of the staff and gossiped worse than a tabloid columnist.

She had nothing to gain by defending herself or acknowledging the waiter's complaint had even the tiniest bit of merit. Nor did she have anything to gain by retaliating. Sooner or later, Tyler would have to face retribution.

Too bad she wouldn't be around to see it.

"Hey, Mr. Prescott." The busboy appeared beside the table. "You want coffee or—"

Sam watched the dazed expression fall over the teenager's face when his eyes dropped to the front of Kiera's damp tank top. The boy's jaw went slack.

"Eddie," Sam prompted.

No response.

Sam sighed. It wasn't that he blamed the kid for staring. Hell, it was all he could do not to stare himself. Kiera was too busy dabbing at her chest to notice that she'd attracted the attention of most of the men in the restaurant.

"Eddie," Sam repeated.

"Huh?" The busboy blinked and looked at Sam.

"The towel?"

"Oh, sure, Mr. Prescott." Eddie grabbed the towel from the waistband of his apron and reached out as if to wipe the front of Kiera's chest.

Sam moved quicker than the boy and grabbed the

towel away. Realizing what he'd almost done, Eddie blushed deeply.

"I think we can manage now, thanks." Sam handed the towel to Kiera. "How 'bout you just bring me that cup of coffee?"

"Sure, Mr. Prescott." Eddie glanced at Kiera and swallowed hard. "You, ah, need anything, miss?"

"I'm fine, thanks." Kiera managed a smile. "I just spilled some lemonade, that's all."

"I—I'll get you some more," he stammered. "You need some water, too? 'Cause I could go get that, case that might stain or something, or maybe you want some club soda—"

"Edward Morrison!" Madge stormed up behind the boy. "Stop drooling over that girl and go get Sam here some coffee."

"Yes, ma'am." Eddie cast one last, puppy-dog look at Kiera.

"Sometime before Christmas?" Madge barked, then shook her head when the boy shuffled off. "What do you think, Sam? You're the big business expert here. Should I fire him?"

"Absolutely."

Kiera's mouth dropped open.

"I'll give him the boot after he brings your coffee." Madge grabbed the pencil she'd stuck over her ear. "The boy's a pain-in-the-butt, anyway. So what'll you have today? The usual?"

"We both will," Sam replied. "Extra cheese."

"Wait—"

"You got it." Madge scribbled on her order pad, then

stuck her pencil behind her ear and snatched up the menu on the table.

Kiera called after the waitress again, but Madge was too busy hollering the order to the cook to hear.

"How could you do such a thing?" Kiera said through clenched teeth. "He's just a kid, a sweet kid, who was just trying to be helpful."

The "sweet" kid reappeared with a mug in one hand and pot of coffee in the other. If he'd been looking at the mug instead of Kiera when he poured, Eddie might have even managed to get some of the coffee in the cup. He jumped when he realized he'd missed, reached for his towel, only to remember he'd given it to Kiera.

"Sorry, Mr. Prescott," Eddie apologized. "I'll be right back."

"I've got it." Kiera was already wiping the spill up. "It was just a drop."

"I'll get another towel," Eddie said and hurried— well, for Eddie it was hurried—off. Sam stared at his empty coffee cup, the mess on the table, then looked back up at Kiera. He gave her an I-told-you-so look.

"Don't you *dare* get that boy fired." She put her hands on the table and leaned forward. Outrage sparked in her blue eyes and flushed her cheeks pink. "You call the owner back here right now and tell her you were just kidding or so help me I'll—"

Kiera stopped suddenly, pressed her mouth into a thin line.

Sam raised an eyebrow. "You'll what?"

He could almost hear Kiera doing battle in her brain.

Her need to defend a slow, clumsy busboy warring with her need to tell her boss off.

"You'll what?" he asked again, lowering his voice. He was dying to know.

"Please." Her fury dissipated like smoke in a breeze. "Please, don't."

He might have strung her along another minute or two, but the desperate look in her eyes, the soft, pleading tone in her voice, took all the fun out of it. "Kiera, Eddie is Madge's son. She fires him at least once a day. Sometimes twice."

"Madge's son?" Kiera glanced at the busboy, who'd already forgotten about bringing a towel and was busy posturing for a cute teenage girl who'd just walked in the front door.

Sam nodded. "The youngest of six boys."

Kiera's eyes widened. "She has *six* boys?"

"Yep." He watched Madge come up behind her son and grab his earlobe, then drag him into the kitchen, lecturing him the whole way. "And she can say whatever she likes about any one of them, but if she hears someone else say anything close to criticism…well, let's just say you wouldn't want to be within ten yards. When her temper's up, the woman moves a lot quicker than you'd think."

"I believe you," Kiera said, then met his gaze. "I…I'm sorry. I guess I got a little carried away."

It struck him how incredibly beautiful she'd looked a moment ago—her face animated with anger, her chin lifted with indignation—and he couldn't stop himself from wondering what all that intensity of emotion and energy would be like in bed.

His bed.

The image of Kiera naked, underneath him, her body arching upward into his—

Madge slid a mug of steaming coffee in front of Sam and frowned. "What is it about teenage boys and hormones that makes them dumb as a post?"

And then she was off again, shaking her head as she walked back to the kitchen, obviously not looking for an answer.

Teenage boys have nothing on us big boys, Sam thought, thankful to have his mind diverted from his fantasy of Kiera. When he glanced at her, he could see she was smiling while she sipped on her lemonade.

He couldn't figure her out. The day she'd dropped the tray of drinks, she wouldn't say one word to defend herself, but today, when she thought that a busboy was going to get the axe, she'd wanted to reach across the table and rip out his liver.

The woman absolutely fascinated him.

"So are you going to tell me?" she asked.

"Tell you?"

"You said there were two complaints."

"Oh, right." In spite of her cool tone, he could see the tension in the rigid line of her shoulders. "Chef Phillipe said you questioned his authority."

"Did he?" Her lips pressed into a thin line.

"Did you?"

She shrugged. "I simply suggested he might have put too much thyme in his chicken kiev."

Sam wasn't certain he'd heard her right. In the two months the replacement chef had been with Adagio's, no one on staff in the restaurant had *ever* questioned him. They wouldn't dare. When it came to his kitchen, the man was a tyrant. "You told Chef Phillipe that he put too much thyme in his chicken?"

"I'm sure it was a mistake," Kiera said.

"You bet it was a mistake."

She frowned. "I meant the chef's mistake."

He stared at her in disbelief. "How do you know he used too much thyme?"

She hesitated, took a long sip of her lemonade. "I could smell it."

"You *smelled* it?" He was amazed that the chef hadn't stuffed Kiera in the pantry and put a double padlock on the door.

"I have an extraordinary sense of smell and taste."

She definitely had an extraordinary smell, Sam thought. From the first moment she'd stepped into the elevator, he'd been captivated by her scent. And her taste...his gaze dropped to her mouth. Right now she'd taste like pink lemonade, and dammit if he didn't want to lick that tart sweetness off those enticing lips. He tried his best not to think about the path the spilled lemonade had taken under her tank top. Tried not to wonder what it would feel like to taste that lemonade on her skin, her breasts...

He tossed back a gulp of coffee, though what he really needed was a tall glass of iced water—poured directly below his belt.

"I'm sorry," she said quietly, carefully setting her glass on the table. "I shouldn't have said anything to Chef Phillipe. I was out of place. I assure you, it won't happen again."

Her contrite tone bothered him much more than anything else she'd said or done. He'd caught a glimpse of the fire simmering just under her surface, an intensity that she clearly kept tamped down.

He wanted to know *why,* dammit. Wanted to know what it was she was so obviously running away from. Why she needed to keep herself so controlled and distant.

It might not be today, he mused.

But he intended to find out.

Four

"Mrs. Carver is just finishing up a phone call, Miss Daniels. Why don't you have a seat?"

Kiera managed a smile at the middle-aged brunette receptionist, then sat stiffly on the tan leather sofa. Afraid that her knees might start knocking, she gripped her thighs and held them tightly.

She was about to meet Clair Carver.

Clair *Blackhawk*.

A knot the size of a trucker's fist twisted in her stomach.

She'd been setting up her lunch station not even ten minutes ago when the restaurant manager, Christine, gave her the message to report to Clair's office. Kiera's first thought was that there'd been more complaints filed against her. Tyler had lightened up a little, but Chef Phillipe had been storming about the kitchen since she'd called him on his faux pas. She'd done her best to keep her opinions to herself, be polite and stay out of the chef's way, but if he wasn't barking orders at her, he was muttering under his breath about mindless, insipid waitresses.

Obviously, the man held a grudge.

Still, Kiera seriously doubted that Clair would handle a problem between a chef and a waitress. Normally, owners didn't get involved in the day-to-day operations of a larger hotel. They had staff for that.

Which led to her second, and definitely more frightening, thought.

Clair knows who I am.

The fist in her stomach twisted tighter.

But how *could* she?

Sam?

As careful as she'd been to cover her tracks, if he'd been curious enough, if he'd dug deep enough and made the right phone calls, it was possible he might have learned who she was. Maybe even why she was here. But it was doubtful. And he certainly hadn't *seemed* curious. Or even interested, for that matter. In fact, for the past four days, since they'd had lunch together at Pappa Pete's, he'd barely even looked at her. She wasn't certain if she was relieved or disappointed.

Both, she decided.

There was no question she was attracted to the man. Butterflies-in-the-stomach attracted. Can't-stop-thinking-about-him attracted.

Fantasy attracted.

When she least expected it, they'd sneak up on her. Those insidious little erotic daydreams. Bare, hot skin against bare, hot skin. Arms and legs intertwined. Busy hands, rushing lips. Sometimes her fantasy involved a bed, sometimes an elevator. In his office—on his desk— was her personal favorite. Sizzling, no-holds-barred sex. Wild. Frantic. Spontaneous. He was as mad for her as she was for him, reaching, gasping...

"Miss Daniels?"

She jumped at the receptionist's voice, blinked quickly. "Yes?"

"Are you all right?" A frown wrinkled the woman's brow. "You look a little flushed."

Darn it! Kiera touched a hand to her cheek, felt the warmth there grow warmer still. "Do I?"

The receptionist nodded. "I heard there might be something going around."

Knowing the effect Sam had on women, Kiera didn't doubt there was a lot of what she had going around. "I'm fine, thank you. Really."

"Miss Daniels, I'm so sorry to keep you waiting."

Kiera froze at the sound of the feminine voice behind her. It was one thing to *imagine* meeting Clair, quite another to actually *do* it.

Breath held, heart pounding, Kiera slowly turned.

Thick, dark brown hair skimmed the shoulders of her lime-colored jacket, framed her high cheekbones and wide mouth. Her skin had the barest kiss of bronze, suggesting her obvious Native American heritage wasn't full-blooded. And her eyes—Kiera stared at Clair's smiling gaze—they were blue. Deep blue.

"Thank you for coming." Clair moved into the room. "I'm Clair Carver."

Kiera watched the woman close the distance between them and felt a moment of panic. *Trey was right. I never should have come here. No good could possibly come of it.* She rose too quickly, awkwardly accepted the hand Clair offered.

"A pleasure to meet you, Mrs. Carver."

"Mrs. Carver," Clair repeated dreamily, her lips curving wider. "Even after six weeks of marriage, I haven't quite gotten used to the sound of it. But please, call me Clair."

Kiera managed a weak smile and nodded. "Kiera."

"Mary—" Clair glanced at the slender gold watch on her wrist "—why don't you take your lunch now? I can handle things by myself here for a little while."

"Mr. Carver told me not to—"

"Never mind what Jacob told you." Softly scolding, Clair tilted her head. "I'm feeling fine now and you both need to stop worrying about me."

Shaking her head in defeat, the receptionist slid her glasses off and picked up her purse. "I'll be back in thirty minutes."

"You'll be back in one hour, not one minute before, or I'll tell Albert in Shipping that you have a crush on him."

"I most certainly do not!" Mary puffed up like an agitated hen, then lowered her brow with worry. "You wouldn't, would you?"

"One hour," Clair said firmly, then smiled at Kiera. "After you."

The spacious inner office, a mix of contemporary and

Western decor, was warm and welcoming. Native American–themed watercolors and bronze statues decorated the walls and shelves. A smooth granite fountain bubbled softly in one corner, and two ficus trees flanked the floor-to-ceiling glass window that overlooked the pool and courtyard.

"Please, sit." Clair waved a hand toward one of the tan leather armchairs in front of a glass-topped cherry-wood desk. "Can I get you something to drink? Some coffee or water? I have some tea, if you like chamomile."

Kiera took the chair closest to the door. "No, thank you."

"I'm sorry I pulled you away from your shift." Clair sat at her desk. "I know how busy the restaurant gets at lunch."

If she's going to lecture or fire me, Kiera thought, *she certainly is being polite about it.* "Not for another half hour."

"Normally, I would have come down and introduced myself to you right away, but I've been a little under the weather for the past few days."

She did look a little tired, Kiera thought, and her cheeks were slightly pale. "I hope it's nothing serious."

"I seem to be over the worst of it now." Leaning back in her chair, Clair narrowed her eyes. "Have we met before?"

Kiera tensed, but managed to keep her tone calm. "Have you ever been to Rainville?"

"Rainville? I don't think so." Clair shook her head thoughtfully. "You look so…familiar, though I'm not sure why."

"I probably just look like someone else."

"Maybe." There was still doubt in Clair's voice, but she shrugged it off. "Anyway, I don't want to keep you, so I should get to the point. I received a phone call regarding you this morning."

Oh, God, she *does* know, Kiera thought. But with her throat closing up on her, she couldn't have spoken if she'd tried.

"Apparently," Clair said, "you've impressed my sister-in-law."

"Your sister-in-law?"

"One of them." Clair smiled. "Grace is married to Rand. She comes here for lunch quite often. You've waited on her a couple of times this past week. She couldn't stop talking about how terrific you are. I decided I wanted to meet you myself."

That's why Clair had called her here? Because her sister-in-law had said something nice about her? Kiera felt a bubble of hysterical laughter threaten to rise, but she quickly swallowed it back down. "I—I appreciate that. But really, I'm just doing my job."

"According to Grace, you were doing much more than your—"

Clair stopped suddenly, raised a hand to her temple and closed her eyes.

"Mrs. Carver?" Kiera leaned forward. "Are you all right?"

"I—I thought I was," she said breathlessly. "But maybe not."

Kiera stood. "I'll get your receptionist."

"No!" Clair opened her eyes and held up her hand. "No, please."

"I really should—"

"Just give me a minute." Clair laid her head back. "It's nothing, just a little wave of nausea. I'll be fine."

"You don't look fine." Her own nervousness forgotten, Kiera spotted a pitcher of water sitting on a console, hurried over and filled a glass, then quickly moved to Clair's side. "In fact, you're quickly approaching the color of your jacket, which I love, by the way. Vera Wang?"

Clair smiled weakly and nodded. "I did a little shopping on my honeymoon."

"Just sip." Kiera held out the glass, studied Clair's face for a moment, then, without thinking, asked, "How far along are you?"

"Far along?" Clair stared blankly at her. "What do you mean?"

Darn it! Why did she have to always speak before she thought? One more thing Trey was right about.

"Nothing. Here, just sip on this."

"You thought I was pregnant?"

Afraid to answer, Kiera shifted uneasily.

"I'm not pregnant." Clair laughed and shook her head. "I just had a little bug last week and I can't seem to shake it. My nephews had it, too."

Mentally kicking herself, Kiera forced a smile and started to back away. "It probably is just a bug. There's always something going around." *Like foot-in-mouth-disease.* "I appreciate you inviting me up here, but I should probably get back to work now."

"Wait." Clair reached out and grabbed Kiera's arm. "Why—what made you think that?"

"I was way out of line," Kiera said, wishing she could

be anywhere but here at this moment. "Of course you'd know if you were pregnant. Just forget I said anything."

Clair's hand tightened on Kiera's arm. "I'm not upset or offended. Really, I'm not. Please, just tell me what made you think that?"

Since it was too late to take the words back or escape, Kiera simply sighed and resigned herself to her fate.

"Well," Kiera said hesitantly, "I've been around a lot of pregnant women. The last restaurant I worked in, three of the servers there were expecting at the same time. They all had that same pale-green tint in their face as you do, the same unexpected wave of nausea that would come and go. I guess I just got pretty good at recognizing 'the look.'"

"And I—" Clair bit her lip "—I have that look?"

Kiera slowly nodded.

"Oh, my God." Clair sank back into her chair. Wide-eyed, she stared blankly out the window. "It's possible. There was that one time…"

Clair's gaze flashed back to Kiera. "Please don't say anything about this to anyone. I want to be sure, and if I am I have to tell Jacob first."

Kiera nodded, couldn't help but note the irony of the situation. "Of course."

"Oh, no—" the green tint in Clair's face deepened "—here it comes again." She slapped her fingers to her mouth and jumped up. "I'll be right back, don't leave. Please don't leave."

Clair didn't wait for an answer, just hurried to a door at the back of her office and ran through it.

Kiera rolled her head back and groaned softly. The

last thing she'd wanted to do was call attention to herself, but, between doing her job well and having a loose tongue, she'd practically screamed to be noticed.

With a heavy sigh, she started to turn and sit back down, but a grouping of silver framed photographs on Clair's shelves caught her attention.

Family photos.

Almost afraid to look, but knowing she had to, Kiera moved closer. There were several pictures, but one of them practically leaped off the shelf at her. Her pulse quickened as she picked up the photo and stared at it. Clair sat on the top rail of a corral fence; two men stood on either side. One of the men Kiera recognized—Rand Blackhawk. They were all smiling, not a posed smile, but one of those shots where someone with a camera sneaks up and captures the essence of the moment on film.

Kiera's fingers tightened on the frame. All three shared the same golden, bronzed skin, the same high cheekbones. The same thick, dark hair.

So familiar. So incredibly familiar.

Beyond William Blackhawk's obituary, Kiera hadn't been able to find out anything about the Blackhawk family. It wasn't as if it was a subject that came up with the few people she'd had contact with in this town. If she started asking questions, there was no doubt in her mind she'd draw unwanted attention. Of course, she'd *already* done that in spades.

"Hi."

Kiera whirled at the sound of Sam's deep voice close behind her. The photo slipped from her hands as she turned, and she could do nothing to stop its descent. She watched the frame bounce off the plush carpeting, then fall open, spilling the glass, the back cover and the photo onto the floor.

Horrified, Kiera dropped to her knees.

"Sorry." Sam knelt beside her, reached for the frame as she reached for the photo. "I guess you didn't hear me knock. I thought Clair was in here."

"She is—she was—she'll be back shortly." Carefully, she lifted the overturned photo, stared at the names hand-written on the back: Rand, Lizzie, Seth, at the Double B.

"Lizzie?"

She hadn't meant to speak out loud, but the name slipped out.

"Clair's birth name is Elizabeth Blackhawk." Sam slid the glass back into the frame. "Her parents died when she was little and she was adopted by a family in South Carolina."

Her parents died when she was little... Kiera let the words sink in. "Clair was adopted?"

"It's a little complicated." Sam took the picture from her, dropped the picture and backing into the frame and held it up. "There we go. No damage done."

No damage done? If only that were true. She couldn't seem to stop the sudden, uncontrollable shaking. She had another piece of the puzzle now, but the picture still made no sense.

"Hey." Frowning, Sam set the frame back on the shelf and took hold of her arms. "It's all right."

It wasn't all right, she thought. Nothing was right. It had nothing to do with a dropped frame, but she couldn't tell him that.

And why did she suddenly want to?

Because she was weary of the charade. Of the lies. Of feeling so damn alone.

Through the fabric of her blouse, she felt the warmth of his large hands, felt his strength. This was crazy. More like *insane*. Kneeling on the floor in Clair's office, Sam's fingers wrapped around her arms. So close…so damn close…

Lifting her gaze to his, she met the intensity of his eyes.

His hands tightened on her arms, his mouth flattened into a hard, thin line. She couldn't breathe, was afraid if she did she'd lose this moment she so badly needed.

Time slowed; her heart raced. She heard everything around her: the quiet ripple of water from the fountain; the faint tick of a desk clock; the distant laughter of children by the pool downstairs. The sounds surrounded her, enclosed her in a world of her own. A world where nothing else existed but her and this man she'd been fantasizing about for days.

Of course, none of her fantasies had been on the floor in Clair's office, she thought dimly. But even that didn't seem to hinder the response she was having to Sam's touch.

This was *so* wrong, so *completely* inappropriate, and even that didn't seem to stop her from wanting this. From wanting him.

Sam's hands tightened even more firmly on her arms; a muscle jumped at the corner of one eye. He made a low, angry sound, then dropped his mouth on hers.

The moment his lips covered hers, right or wrong or

inappropriate was no longer an issue. Nothing mattered, nothing at all, other than the feel of his mouth on hers.

She tasted his frustration, his anger. His need. He crushed his lips over hers, demanding, insistent. Sensations ripped through her, overwhelming, intense. Her hands clutched his suit lapels, fisted. She leaned into him, into the sheer desire gripping her. Her fantasies had been *nothing* compared to this. Not even close. How could they have been?

Sam jerked his head back and loosened his grip on her. "Kiera."

Dazed, and definitely confused, she slowly opened her eyes. His face appeared to be cut in steel, his narrowed gaze fierce. He rose, pulling her with him, then dropped his hands from her arms.

She stared at him, struggled to gain the control that he'd so easily attained. Knowing that she'd practically begged him to kiss her, she felt like a fool.

"I—I'm sorry," she said, but her heart was still pounding hard, her breath still frayed. "I—"

"Sorry I took so long." Clair stepped back into the office, stopped short. "Oh, Sam, you're early."

"I didn't realize you were with someone." Calmly, he bent and retrieved the frame still lying on the carpet. "I'll come back."

"That's not necessary." Kiera felt the heat of her blush on her cheeks, watched Clair glance curiously between her and Sam. "I was just leaving."

"Actually, Kiera…" Clair said, her tone reserved "…if you don't mind, I need another minute of your time."

Dammit! Kiera bit the inside of her lip. As if it wasn't

bad enough she'd made a fool out of herself with Sam, she was about to get a reprimand on employee-employer relationships. "All right."

"Thank you." Clair glanced at Sam. "We won't be long."

He hesitated, then reluctantly turned and left the room.

Kiera squared her shoulders and faced Clair.

"You said you lived in a small town, didn't you?" Clair asked.

Not exactly what Kiera had expected Clair to say. "Yes."

Clair moved to the window and stared down at the pool. "Working at the Four Winds, being here day in and day out, it's just like a small town. We all get to know each other very well. Maybe a little too well."

Here it comes… Kiera held her breath.

"It's not easy when everyone knows your business," Clair said. "Sometimes even before you know it."

How well Kiera understood—and agreed with—that. But she simply nodded.

"I realize this is an imposition." Biting her lip, Clair turned. A mixture of fear and hope lit her eyes. "But I need to ask a favor of you."

Five

Sam sat in his car and stared at the Shangri-La's brilliant pink neon sign. Like the beat of a song, the last two letters flickered steadily, blinking in and out...*La*...*La*...*La*...grating on his nerves. He tapped impatiently on his steering wheel.

Where the *hell* was she?

It was seven-fifteen, for God's sake. He knew her lunch shift had ended almost two hours ago. On the hotel security monitor, he'd watched her walk to her white sedan in the employee garage and drive away. Even with a traffic jam—which was virtually nonexistent in Wolf River—it wouldn't have taken her more than five minutes to drive here.

Dammit.

Heat lingered from the blistering day and radiated off

the asphalt parking lot, cutting a sharper edge on his foul mood. *You've gotten soft, Prescott,* he told himself irritably. When he'd been in the Army, he'd run reconnaissance in a South American jungle, where mosquitoes were big enough to throw a saddle on and the humidity was so thick you could drink it. He'd lain patiently in bug-infested swamps for hours, even dodged a few bullets.

If he could, he'd take those swamps and bullets over sitting here in this damn car, in this damn parking lot, any day.

He swiped at the sweat on his brow, thankful he'd at least changed into a T-shirt and jeans before he'd driven over here. Even after eight years in the hotel business, he'd never completely got used to the daily suit-and-tie routine. But, like the Army, he knew it was the uniform for the job so he dealt with it.

He glanced at his wristwatch again, was annoyed that only two minutes had passed since the last time he'd looked.

La...La...La...

He tapped harder, gritted his teeth, then looked up when he heard the crunch of gravel under tires. A white sedan had pulled into the motel driveway. *About damn time.* He reached for his keys, swore when he saw the driver of the car. Male, balding, thick glasses. Big nose.

Wrong white sedan.

With a heavy sigh, he settled back again, seriously considered leaving, going back to the motel and having a good stiff drink at the bar. Forget that today had ever happened.

Right. Nothing short of death or complete amnesia could make him forget he'd kissed Kiera.

It infuriated him he'd lost control like that. Stepped over—hell, *jumped* over—all boundaries. He'd been so damn careful to stay away from her the past few days. Had made a point not to speak to her, or even look in her direction, for that matter. And then in the blink of an eye, he'd blown his hard-won restraint to smithereens.

What the hell was he supposed to do when she'd looked up at him with those sexy blue eyes? When she'd softly parted those enticing lips? When she'd swayed toward him. Walk away?

Hell, yes.

That's *exactly* what he should have done.

Frowning, he raked his fingers over his scalp. In spite of what some people thought, he *was* human.

And *stupid,* he thought darkly. Not only because he'd kissed her, but because—of all places—he'd kissed her in Clair's office.

Clair hadn't said word to suggest she'd seen, or suspected anything had happened between Kiera and him. But during their meeting with the Four Winds architect, when they'd been studying the blueprints for the new tower, Sam had caught Clair—more than once—staring blankly across the table. As if her mind were somewhere far away.

Sam knew his lack of protocol could potentially put Clair and the hotel's reputation in an awkward situation. Sexual harassment claims and lawsuits were hardly good for business. Because he'd never stepped over that boundary before, it had never been an issue for him.

Until Kiera.

He wished he knew what it was about the woman that intrigued him to the point of distraction. She was pretty—beautiful, even. And sexy, for damn sure. He wished the attraction were as simple as that. If it were, it would pass quickly enough. But something, some little, annoying itch between his shoulder blades, told him it was more than that. Much more.

He sighed, sank down farther in his seat. Maybe it was the mystery surrounding her, he thought. Maybe when he'd seen that black eye, some primal need to protect had been awakened. Or maybe he'd simply been without female companionship longer than he was accustomed to. Of all the reasons, he preferred that one. It was the easiest to rectify.

He straightened suddenly, spotted her across the parking lot, getting out of her car, her arms loaded with brown grocery bags. She'd driven right past him and he hadn't even seen her!

So much for his reconnaissance expertise.

By the time he came up behind her, she had her key in her hand and was juggling the bags in her arms while she reached to unlock her door.

"I'll get it."

With a gasp, she jerked her head up and stared wide-eyed at him. "Sam!"

He took the bags from her, nodded at the door when she just stood there, staring at him. "You going to open it?"

"What? Oh, yes." It took her a moment to fit the key into the lock. When she opened the door, she turned and blocked the doorway, reached for the bags. "This really isn't a good time, maybe you can—"

"I'm coming in, Kiera."

She hesitated, then stepped to the side.

The room was spacious, with a small kitchenette, chrome dining table, box-shaped tweed sofa and a rust-colored armchair. Over the sofa, a large, framed print of a sunny, palm tree–lined beach attempted—unsuccessfully—to brighten up the drab room. An open door to the right of the sofa led to the bedroom.

He jerked his gaze away. The last thing he wanted to think about right now was the bedroom.

He set the groceries on the Formica kitchen counter, caught the scent of fresh herbs wafting from one of the bags, noticed two wine bottles in another. "Are you expecting company?"

She stood by the still-open door, white-knuckling the doorknob. "Why do you ask?"

"Why are you answering a question with a question?"

At the sound of a car pulling into a parking space close by, Kiera quickly glanced outside, then shut the door. "Just because I'm cooking doesn't mean I'm expecting anyone."

Again, she hadn't answered his question. "You have two bottles of wine."

She arched an eyebrow. "Are you the wine police?"

When he frowned at her, she sighed, then moved into the kitchen and lifted a bottle of cheap Bordeaux out of the bag.

"One's for drinking, one's for cooking." She plucked a corkscrew out of a drawer. "Why don't you just tell me why you're here."

"All right." He watched her effortlessly open the bottle. The dark, tangy scent of the red wine drifted across the counter. "I want to know if you'd like to file a complaint."

"Yes, I would." She pulled a frying pan out of a cupboard under the stovetop. "This frying pan is too small."

"Dammit, Kiera." He narrowed his eyes. "You know what I mean."

"Assuming you're referring to our little breach of conduct this afternoon, of course I don't want to file a complaint." She set the pan on the stove and met his gaze. "Sam, we're both adults. What happened…just happened, that's all."

"That's all you have to say?" he said tightly. "'It just happened?'"

"What do you want me to say?" With a shrug, she fumbled in one of the bags, pulled out fresh herbs, butter and an onion.

What *did* he want her to say? he wondered. Her answer should have relieved, not annoyed him. If he had half a brain, he'd be done with this, with *her,* and get the hell out now.

Apparently, he wasn't that smart.

"I kissed you, Kiera," he said, stating the obvious. "I shouldn't have."

"Because you're my boss?"

"Of course because I'm your boss." His annoyance increased when she didn't answer him but grabbed a knife instead and sliced off a chunk of butter, then dropped it into the pan.

"And what if you weren't my boss?" she said casually, then reached for the basil.

His pulse jumped at her comment. He couldn't tell if she was playing one of those coy, female games, or if she was seriously asking him a question. He watched her chop the basil, smelled the pungent scent of the spice filling the room. *Dammit! Why can't I read her?*

"If I wasn't your boss," he said slowly, evenly, "I'd have done a hell of a lot more than kiss you."

In spite of her resolve to be nonchalant, Kiera couldn't stop the winged stutter in her heart. She shouldn't have asked him that, knew her question was playing with fire. But somehow the words had just slipped out, and there was no taking them back now.

And if—for once—she was going to be truthful, she didn't want to take them back.

Her stomach jumped when he moved around the counter toward her. She didn't look at him, didn't dare. If she did, he'd certainly see everything she was thinking. Everything she was feeling. She wasn't ready for that. *Not yet,* she thought. It was too soon.

"Are you thinking about quitting?" He moved closer. "Or are you suggesting something else?"

Something else? She glanced up sharply as she realized what he meant, felt her cheeks warm. She supposed her question *did* sound like some kind of a proposition to have a secret affair or be a kept woman. She lifted her chin. "Of course I'm not suggesting anything else."

"What if I did?"

She stilled at his words, not certain if she should be insulted or excited. "What if you did what?"

"For starters—" he reached down and took the knife from her hand, laid it on the cutting board, then reached for her "—this."

His mouth covered hers. A hot, hungry kiss that stole her breath, sent her pulse racing and her mind spinning. And there it was again. Absolute pleasure, intense need. It streaked through her like liquid lightning, setting her skin on fire. She met the moist heat of his tongue with her own, slid her hands up the rock-solid wall of his chest. A moan rose from deep in her throat, hummed through her entire body. She was powerless to stop it, so she gave herself up to the feeling, let it melt through and consume her.

Wonderful, she thought, wrapping her arms around his neck.

So wonderfully wonderful.

He dragged her closer, deepened the kiss, maneuvered her between him and the Formica counter. She reveled in the feel of his hard, powerful body pressed tightly against hers. No one had ever kissed her like this before. Had ever made her feel such raw, wild need. It frightened and thrilled her at the same time. The kiss this afternoon had simply been an appetizer, she realized, a precursor to the main course.

She clutched at his back, rose on her toes to get closer.

Shifting his weight, he slid his hands down her spine and cupped her bottom. She heard a deep, low growl in his throat, then gasped when he suddenly lifted her up onto the counter and stepped between her legs. The paper bag behind her spilled over, and through the blood pounding in her head, she vaguely heard the oranges she'd bought roll onto the floor and bounce. She didn't care. With Sam's kisses spinning her world out of control, how could she?

His mouth left hers and she whimpered, drew in a sharp breath as his lips blazed kisses over her jaw to her ear. She rolled her head back, bit her lip when his teeth nipped her earlobe, then moved to her neck. Fire raced over her skin, pulsated at the juncture of her thighs. His lips and teeth teased and explored, but his mouth wasn't the only part of him that was busy. His hands worked her shirt from her waistband, then quickly slid underneath.

She quivered, lost herself to the mind-numbing sensations of his skin on hers. His palms were rough and when they cupped her breasts, she arched her back. He mumbled something, lowered his head to nuzzle. Gasping, she braced her arms on the counter behind her, and in some dim recess of her mind felt the small, plastic-wrapped box under her fingers.

And remembered what she'd bought.

When she stiffened, he raised his head.

"What?" he asked, his voice husky and deep.

"Nothing." She closed her hand around the box, tried to push it back into the paper bag, but the bag moved away and fell on the floor.

Oh, hell.

With a frown, he straightened and glanced behind her back.

She watched his eyes narrow, then his mouth press into a hard line when he saw what was in the box.

A pregnancy test.

His gaze shot back to hers. "You're *pregnant?*"

If the situation—and the look in Sam's eyes—hadn't been so intense, she might have laughed at the absurdity of his question. She certainly didn't want him to think the test was for her, but she couldn't very well tell him that Clair had asked her to buy it, either. No matter what Sam thought of her, Kiera wouldn't break that trust.

When she didn't reply, he stepped back and dragged a hand through his rumpled hair. "Dammit, Kiera, I can't help you if you won't talk to me."

She slid off the counter, picked the bag up from the floor, then dropped the box inside. "I didn't ask you for help, Sam."

His eyes dark with anger, he stared at her for what felt like a lifetime.

"Fine."

He ground the single word out through gritted teeth, then turned and headed for the door. He yanked it open, stopped, spun around and leveled his gaze at her.

"Just tell me this," he said tightly. "And dammit, tell me the truth. Are you married?"

That she could honestly answer. "No."

A muscle jumped in his clenched jaw. She watched him turn and slam out the door. Slowly, she released the breath she'd been holding, then leaned against the counter and closed her eyes.

She heard a car engine rev, then the squeal of tires.

Men!

With an irritated groan, she pushed away from the counter and bent to pick up the fruit that had rolled on the floor. Why should *he* be mad at *me?* she thought, picking up an orange and tossing it back onto the counter. And why were the men in her life who mattered to her most so damn demanding?

She scooped up another orange and glared at it. "I *refuse* to be bullied."

Why the hell did she have to fall for a guy who had the same ornery, the same intolerable, the same insufferable temperament as Trey?

She spun around at the sudden knock on the door. So he'd come back to interrogate her further, she thought and marched toward the door, ready to argue if that's what he wanted. She threw open the door.

But it wasn't Sam standing there. It was Clair.

"I—I'm sorry," Clair said hesitantly, obviously startled at the unexpected force of the door opening. "I must have come at a bad time."

"No, no. Of course not." Kiera felt the heat of a blush scurry up her neck onto her face. "I'm sorry. I thought you were—never mind. Please, come in."

Kiera closed the door when Clair stepped inside, then moved to the counter and picked up the box sitting there. "I hope I bought the right one. There were several to choose from and I really hadn't a clue."

"I wouldn't have known, either." Clair stared at the pregnancy kit with a mixture of wonder and amazement on her face. Tears suddenly filled her eyes. "Oh, I hope you're right. I really, really hope you're right."

"Then I really, really hope I'm right, too," Kiera said, then stiffened when Clair moved forward and hugged her. Just a brief hug, a simple, I'm-just-so-happy-I-want-to-share-it hug.

But to Kiera it was so much more.

It was a hug that had the power to topple defenses. To break through walls. To answer questions.

If there was anyone she dared trust, anyone who might be able to answer those questions, Kiera knew it was Clair.

But she couldn't. Not only because it was terrible timing, but because now that she had established this connection she was terrified of losing it, afraid that the joy shining in Clair's eyes would turn to doubt. Maybe even to hatred.

When the time is right, she thought, praying it would be soon.

"I'm sorry." With a sniff, Clair stepped back and wiped at the tears in her eyes. "I've just been so emotional these past couple of weeks."

"That's another sure sign." Kiera blinked back her own threatening tears, then shifted uneasily, not sure what to do now. "Can I—ah, would you like something to drink? Some water or iced tea?"

"Iced tea would be wonderful," Clair said distantly, still staring at the box in her hands. "I think I might need a couple of minutes to calm down before I drive home."

"Sugar?" Kiera asked, pulling a pitcher out of the fridge.

"No, thanks." Clair moved to the counter, glanced at the groceries and the chopped basil. "You cook?"

"I like to," Kiera said, filling a glass from the cupboard. "Do you?"

"Never learned, and now I'm too busy." Clair nodded at the pan with butter in it. "What are you making?"

"Chicken marsala." Kiera handed the tea to Clair,

then threw caution to the wind. "You're welcome to stay and eat if you're hungry."

"Just the tea, but thanks for the offer. Maybe a rain check?"

"Sure."

"Don't let me keep you, though," Clair said, sipping her tea. "I would enjoy watching you for a few minutes. It fascinates me how people can take a bunch of different ingredients and turn them into something exotic and delicious. Unless you'd rather not have someone hanging over you—"

"I don't mind." Kiera moved back to the stove and flipped on the burner. If there was one place she felt most comfortable, it was in the kitchen. And besides, if she was cooking it would keep her mind off being nervous around Clair—off all those questions she so desperately wanted to ask.

"So where did you learn?" Clair settled on a counter bar stool. "Your mother?"

Kiera shook her head. "Cookie Roggenfelder."

Clair raised a questioning eyebrow.

"I was raised on a ranch in East Texas." Kiera opened a package of chicken breasts she'd had the butcher pound thin for her. "When I was eight, I spent most of my time following after the cook."

"Named Cookie," Clair added, grinning.

Kiera nodded. "I'd beg him every day to let me help and every day he'd say no. I guess I finally wore him down, because on my ninth birthday he gave me an apron and told me if I still wanted to help, I had to start at the bottom. The bottom being peeling potatoes, shucking corn, chopping onions. It was nearly six months before he let me actually cook anything. I made corn fritters."

"How did you do?" Clair asked.

"They were hard as granite and burned, to boot." While she opened a bag of flour, Kiera smiled at the memory. The kitchen had smelled like smoke for three days. "Cookie insisted I bake them every day until I got it right. Took me three weeks straight, but now I can honestly say I make the best corn fritter you've ever tasted."

"I've never had one." Clair swirled the ice in her tea. "But you're definitely making me want one."

"I'll make them for you sometime," Kiera said, then dusted the chicken with flour. "You'll be spoiled for life."

Clair studied Kiera's face for a moment, then took another drink. "Does that mean you'll be staying in Wolf River?"

Kiera's heart jumped a beat. "What do you mean?"

"Like I said before, small towns are brutal on a person's private life." Clair gave an apologetic shrug. "There's been some talk."

"Oh?" Somehow, Kiera managed to keep her hand steady. Butter sizzled when she dropped the chicken into the heated frying pan. "What kind of talk?"

"What you'd expect," Clair said. "Where you come from, why you're here. Why you're living in a motel, by yourself. If you're married."

"I'm not married." But she'd answered a little too quickly, Kiera realized, especially for someone who was trying her damnedest to be calm and collected.

"I'm sorry if I'm prying." Clair's voice was truly contrite. "But I do have an interest in you beyond idle curiosity. I'd like to know if the best waitress my hotel has ever hired plans on sticking around for a while. And besides, I like you. This may sound weird, and it's probably just my hormones going crazy, but I feel as if we have a connection, somehow. I realize we just met, but I'd hate to lose you, as a Four Winds employee, and as a friend."

"I—" Kiera had to choke back the lump of emotion in her throat "—thank you. I don't know what to say."

"Tell me that chicken you're cooking will be done soon," Clair said with a grin. "I wasn't hungry a minute ago and now I'm suddenly starving."

Kiera and Clair looked at each other. Together they said, "Another sign of pregnancy."

They laughed, then Clair folded her arms and leaned forward on the counter. "I promise I won't pry anymore, but I'd love to hear more about Cookie and the ranch you grew up on. It sounds wonderful."

It *had* been wonderful, Kiera thought. Until two weeks ago, when she'd found out everything had been a lie. For the moment, though, she would pretend she didn't know the truth. Meeting Clair had helped ease the pain somewhat, but there was still so much to learn. So many questions to be answered.

And besides, after her incredible lapse of good judgment with Sam, she needed a distraction. Cooking and talking with Clair would certainly be a welcome one.

"My favorite Cookie story—" Kiera said while she

turned the chicken "—has to be the day one of the new ranch hands inadvertently commented that his mama made the best ribs in the entire state of Texas...."

Six

It seemed as if everywhere he turned, Sam saw an expectant mother. In the lobby. On the elevator. At the pool. An hour ago he'd seen *two* of them, walking together into the hotel spa. Then there was Christine, Adagio's manager, three of the women in Housekeeping and two of the desk clerks. Was it some kind of cosmic joke being played on him, or had he just suddenly become excruciatingly aware of their presence?

Scrubbing a hand over his face, he leaned back in his desk chair and stared at the report on his monitor. He'd been staring at the same page, at the same figures, for the past half hour. The way his day was going, he might finish this simple accounting statement around one or two in the morning.

But why should today go any better than last night?

It frustrated—and irritated—the hell out of him he couldn't get Kiera out of his mind. Or the burning question: was she pregnant?

It had taken a will of iron today not to seek her out and force the issue. If she'd thought she was pregnant, it might explain why she'd been so secretive since she got here, especially if she was running away from the father of her child. She'd told him she wasn't married, so the father would most likely be a boyfriend. He remembered the black eye she'd had when she'd first arrived, and his hands tightened on the arms of his chair.

Five minutes, Sam thought, narrowing his eyes. That's all the time he'd need with the guy. Hell, that would be taking it slowly. He could mess the jerk up big-time in under two without breaking a sweat.

He shook his head and sighed. Something just didn't jive here. Not that he knew anything at all about pregnant women. He didn't know a damn thing.

He couldn't put his finger on it, but he had a feeling that what he was seeing, what she'd *let* him see, was all wrong.

Or was that just what he *wanted* to think?

He swore, then rose and walked to the window in his office, stared down at the crowded pool. It was late afternoon, a popular time for guests to swim and stretch out on the lounge chairs. There had to be at least thirty people down there. Kids splashing, old men in shorts with white legs and socks sitting under umbrellas. Gorgeous women sunbathing in bikinis. And where did his eyes end up?

On a pregnant woman.

Dammit!

He turned and started to pace. Kiera was just as attracted to him as he was to her, there was no question about that. She'd been just as wild for him as he'd been for her. God, he could still taste her, still feel her body pressed against his.

He dragged both hands through his hair and linked them behind his head. What the hell was she hiding from him? he wondered. Or, more likely, *who?* Why wouldn't she tell him anything? And why wouldn't she let him help?

She was driving him crazy.

I don't want this complication, he told himself. *I like my life just the way it is.*

So why couldn't he stop thinking about her? Why couldn't he stop worrying if she was all right, if she needed anything?

If the test was positive…

He continued to pace. In spite of his lack of knowledge regarding "female stuff," he just couldn't believe she was pregnant. Kiera hadn't missed a beat since she'd been hired at Adagios. She worked as hard, if not harder, than any other server on staff. Weren't pregnant women supposed to throw up a lot, turn green and sleep all the time?

Shoot, Clair was acting more like she was pregnant than Kiera, he thought. Just yesterday she'd fallen asleep in the middle of a presentation by that publicist for the Cattlemen's Association, and she'd had that bug she hadn't been able to shake—

He stopped, furrowed his brow.

Clair?

Where the hell *had* that thought come from?

Clair *had* been acting strangely the past two days. He'd assumed because she'd suspected something had happened between him and Kiera.

But what if he'd had it all wrong, and she'd been distracted for another reason? Lord knew nothing had been as it seemed since Kiera had shown up. Why should this be any different?

Why indeed?

He squared his shoulders and set his back teeth. Enough already. He wanted answers.

And he wanted them now.

"Imbecile!" A loud clash of pots and pans followed Chef Phillipe's ringing insult. "This is repulsive. *Mon dieu,* I would not feed this slop to the pigs, let alone people."

A plate of grilled salmon in her hand, Kiera listened to Chef Phillipe berate Robert, Adagio's sous-chef. Phillipe was on his usual daily rampage and poor Robert was his most recent victim.

"This is what I think of your so-called food." Phillipe picked up the pan and turned it over, spilling the sauce onto the floor. For good measure, he then tossed the pan on the floor, as well. "You are a disgrace to chefs everywhere."

Red-faced, Robert glanced from the mess to Phillipe. "But I did what you—"

"Silence!" Phillipe bellowed. "Your brain is like a *petite* pea. Who taught you to cook? The man who cleans out your plumbing pipes?"

Kiera winced. While she was grateful that Phillipe's

anger hadn't been turned on her for once, she couldn't help but feel sorry for the young man. He was fresh out of culinary school and from what she'd seen, quite talented, though still unsure of himself. Kiera figured any confidence that Robert had would quickly be beaten out of him by Phillipe.

Stay out of it, she told herself. *Just turn around and walk away.*

"Must I do everything myself?" Phillipe towered menacingly over Robert, who was visibly shaking. "You are incompetent."

She clamped her teeth together and turned away. *Haven't you got enough problems of your own? This is your last order of the day. Just keep walking…*

"You will never be a chef," Phillipe continued. "You are not even fit to serve the food that I prepare."

Unable to help herself, Kiera glanced over her shoulder, saw Robert's eyes welling up.

Oh, hell.

She sucked in a breath, let a heartbeat pass, then dropped the plate in her hand. Well, more like *threw* the plate, she supposed. It landed with a loud, satisfying shatter.

Phillipe spun around, his eyes bulging with fury.

"Sorry," she said innocently. "It slipped."

Launching into his native language, Phillipe rounded on her, his fists clenched. Kiera spoke, and understood, enough French to know that his insults were as vile as they were insulting. The man was an ass, and she knew she should probably back away—or at least be afraid—but anger overrode her good sense.

And the expression on poor Robert's face—a mix of horror and relief—was enough to make her stand her ground.

If there was one thing Trey had taught her, Kiera thought, it was how to drop a man—any size—to the floor. When Phillipe strode toward her, she waited for the man to even lift a finger. Almost hoped that he would. With all the frustration that had been building in her since she'd left Stone Ridge Ranch, she was certain her knee would pack quite a wallop.

When Phillipe moved into her space, she tightened her leg—

"What the hell is going on here?"

Kiera froze at the sound of Sam's voice behind her. Dammit! Would this man forever be sneaking up on her?

Still, she didn't turn, didn't take her eyes off Phillipe, who looked as if he was about to pop a blood vessel in that thick neck of his.

"What is *wrong?*" His chest heaving, Phillipe glared at Sam. "I will *tell* you what is wrong. I am surrounded by complete idiots."

From the corner of her eye, Kiera watched Sam's jaw tighten. He glanced at Robert and the mess at his feet, then the plate she'd dropped. When he lifted his gaze back to her, she saw the controlled anger there. Her spine stiffened. *Believe whatever you want,* she thought. He'd already tried and convicted her yesterday when he'd seen the pregnancy test. What possible difference could it make to add one more crime to her long list of offenses?

"He is a buffoon." Phillipe pointed a sausage-thick

finger at Robert, then narrowed his beady eyes at Kiera. "And she is a clumsy, insolent—"

"That's enough."

The chef puffed up his chest. "You cannot expect me to work with such dim-witted, *abruti*—"

"I said, that's *enough.*"

Stunned at the steel-edged tone in Sam's voice, Phillipe clamped his mouth shut and gave an indignant tug at the hem of his shirt. "I will return in fifteen minutes. I expect them both to be gone."

Phillipe turned on his heels and stomped out of the kitchen. Sam turned his gaze to the trembling sous-chef. "Robert, go over to catering and help Andrew with the anniversary party in the ballroom."

"I'm not fired?" Robert asked incredulously.

"You're not fired." A muscle jumped in Sam's clenched jaw. "Just don't let Phillipe see you until I straighten this out."

"Yes, sir." Robert hesitated, then cast an anxious glance at Kiera. She smiled reassuringly at him. He smiled back weakly and hurried out of the kitchen.

When Sam turned his dark gaze on her, Kiera pressed her lips firmly together. She refused to make excuses or apologize. "I dropped a plate."

"Did you?" He looked down at the broken china and food, then back at her. "Come with me."

Her heart sank. *Damn you!* she wanted to scream. How could he have kissed her like he had—twice!—and suddenly treat her with such cold disregard? Did he even care what had happened here?

Did he care about her?

Apparently not.

"What about my customer's order?" Kiera glanced at the salmon she'd intentionally dropped on the floor, then thought about the sweet, white-haired woman who'd ordered it. "I can't just leave."

"I'll have a menu and apology sent over and comp the meal."

"It took her twenty minutes to decide on the salmon." Kiera knew she was goading him, she was beyond caring. "I doubt that will make her happy."

"Fine." He could have ground glass between his clenched jaw. "I'll comp a meal for two and if she's a guest here, I'll comp her room, too. Will that make her happy?"

"I'm sure it will." Delighted that *something* good was going to come of this debacle, Kiera gave a satisfied nod. "You sure you don't want me to finish up my shift, because it's almost over and—"

"No, Kiera, I don't want you to finish up your shift. One of the other servers can cover your station. Now *come with me.*"

He turned and slammed through the kitchen's double doors. On the other side, the entire lunch staff scattered like a herd of frightened deer.

Kiera yanked her apron off and threw it on a counter. He wanted to talk to her? Fine.

She'd *talk* all right.

Pushing through the doors, she grabbed her purse out of the employee closet. After she told Sam Prescott exactly what she thought of him, it was pretty much a done deal she'd get canned. The last thing she wanted was to have to come back here and deal with the you-poor-thing-you-didn't-deserve-it condolences. Strangely enough, even Tyler was looking at her with sympathy.

She caught up with Sam after he'd paused long enough to give instructions to Christine, then followed him through the restaurant.

He didn't say one word to her.

In the elevator, she stared straight ahead, refused to even glance at Sam, determined to hold her tongue until they were in the privacy of his office. She'd been holding in too much for too long. She was ready—past ready—to let it out. No doubt she'd regret it later, but she'd simply deal with that when the time came.

Tension crackled in the tiny space, and the overhead music sounded like a muted roar. When the doors slid quietly open, Sam strode purposefully into the hallway without giving her so much as a glance. Part of his intimidation method, she figured, stalking after him. She kept her gaze lasered to the back of his head, every step heightening her already strained emotions.

He stopped outside an unmarked office, slid a card-key into the door and opened it, then stepped aside. Head high, she marched in. When she heard the door close behind her, she dropped her purse onto an armchair and whirled on him.

"Chef Phillipe is a bully," she said furiously. "He insults every member of the staff and refuses to acknowledge any mistake on his part, though let me tell you, he makes plenty."

Arms folded, Sam simply stared at her.

A tiny little voice told her to put a sock in it, but she

squashed the voice like a bug. She was on a roll and had no intention of slowing down.

"The man hasn't a creative bone in his body," she ranted on. "Everyone knows he's hanging on the skill and reputation of your last chef. Everyone but you, obviously, or you wouldn't put up with his arrogant nonsense."

Sam lifted an eyebrow. "Is that so?"

"Yes, that's so." She slammed her hands onto her hips and moved closer. "Robert is a wonderful sous-chef and he has tremendous potential. He just needs a little guidance, which he'll never get from Phillipe. You know why?"

"I have the feeling you're going to tell me," Sam said evenly.

"Yes, I am going to tell you." Why not? she thought. She'd already cooked her goose, why not serve it on a platter while she was at it? "Because any sign of talent threatens him so he beats it down. Because he knows he lacks the *je ne sais quoi* that a truly great chef is born with. And because, sooner or later, he knows that he'll be found out, and when he is he'll be flipping burgers and slinging hash in a coffee shop somewhere."

Lord, but she was riled.

Sam watched Kiera throw her arms out in exaspera-tion. Her cheeks were flushed and sparks flew from her eyes like tiny blue bolts of lightning. He was certain he'd never met anyone like this woman before. She abso-lutely fascinated him.

She absolutely dazzled him.

"I don't know why I'm trying to explain this to you.

You wouldn't understand working in a kitchen, what it means, what it takes." She spun on her heels and flounced away. "And why should you believe anything I say, anyway? You're too busy making assumptions and passing judgments."

"Kiera—"

"You're management, I'm just a waitress. What the hell do *I* know?"

"Kiera—"

"I'm done talking. So what are you waiting for? Fire me already." She whirled around and faced him. "Never mind. I'll make your job easy. I quit."

"Kiera," he said patiently. "I believe you."

That stopped her. "What?"

"I said, I believe you."

"You do?"

"Yes."

Still unsure, she tilted her head. "Which part?"

Sam folded his arms and sighed. "Chef Phillipe is a bully riding on the previous chef's coattails," he repeated her words. "He hasn't a creative bone in his body and Robert is a good sous-chef. I already knew all that."

"You did?"

"Yes, I did."

She frowned. "So then why did you let me go on like that?"

Grinning, he leaned back against the door. "I was enjoying the show."

Her frown darkened, then she suddenly went still and scanned around the room, confused. "This isn't your office."

He was wondering how long it would take her to notice. "No, this is not my office."

She took in the living room area of the large suite and the kitchen. "This is your…ah, where you…"

"Live," he finished for her.

She glanced back at him. "I don't understand."

"I wanted privacy." He saw her breath catch when he pushed away from the door.

She shifted awkwardly. "I hardly think dragging me out of the kitchen in front of the entire staff is private."

"Would you have come up here with me if I'd told you where we were going?"

"I—no."

The beat she'd waited to answer was just long enough to make his pulse jump. She wouldn't have said no, and they both knew it.

Yet still, he could see the inner war waging in her eyes: stand her ground or bolt. She was already running away from something or someone in her life. He had no intention of letting her run away from him.

Not anymore.

But she didn't bolt, just stood still, kept her gaze level as he closed the distance between them until he was less than an arm's reach away.

"You're not pregnant."

She jerked her head up. "What?"

"You're not pregnant. You bought that test for someone else."

"And why would I do that?"

She was on guard now. He'd come to recognize the look in her eyes when he approached a subject she clearly did not want to talk about. "Because Clair asked you to."

"She *told* you that?"

He shook his head. "She didn't tell me anything. It's more of an uneducated guess. You just confirmed it."

Her eyes narrowed sharply. "You tricked me."

"I didn't trick you," he stated. "I'm simply trying to understand why Clair would ask someone she's just met to buy a pregnancy test for her."

"I really don't see where that's any concern of yours."

"Fine." He shrugged and started to turn. "I'll just go ask her myself."

"No!"

Sam turned back, watched her chew on the inside of her lip while she struggled with the proverbial rock and hard place situation.

"She had all the signs," Kiera said finally. "I just sort of suggested she might be pregnant. She hadn't considered the possibility until I asked her how far along she was."

He raised a questioning eyebrow. "And she asked you to buy a pregnancy test for her?"

"If she'd bought it herself, how long do you think it would take for the entire town to find out?"

"Probably not even long enough for the stick to turn blue."

"Exactly."

"So did it?"

She started to say something, then quickly pressed her lips together.

He grinned. "Now *that* was trying to trick you."

"Whether she is or she isn't, and who she wants to tell

when, is Clair's decision," Kiera said primly. "And I'd appreciate you not mentioning this conversation to her."

"Geez, I don't know." He shook his head doubtfully. "This is pretty big news. It just might innocently slip out, you know, when I'm distracted or caught up in work."

"Sam, please," she said anxiously and reached out. "Don't joke about this. Clair trusted me to keep this quiet."

He glanced down at the hand she'd laid on his arm, wondered how the hell such a simple, innocent touch could make his blood rush. "I think I can manage to refrain from spreading gossip and rumors."

Relief washed over her face, then she quickly pulled her hand from his arm and stepped back. "I—I'm sorry. I didn't mean to imply you would be anything but discreet. Obviously, you've already proven that you are."

He knew she was talking about herself now, not Clair. "I've also proven I jump to conclusions."

Linking her hands together, she glanced down at the floor. "If I *had* been, I mean, if I *were* pregnant, would you have, would it…"

When her voice trailed off, he moved closer, lowered his voice. "Would it have mattered?"

She lifted her head. "Yes."

"You don't know?" he asked quietly.

She shook her head. "The only thing I know is that I'm attracted to you, and I think you're attracted to me."

Attracted? He let the word roll around his brain for a moment. It seemed like such a mild description for what he felt toward her. Other words came to his mind…*need, desperate, insane.*

He lifted his hand and cupped her chin in his palm,

felt her tremble at his touch. "I have three rules I live by," he said softly, watched her eyes slowly close when he ran his thumb over her soft cheek. "Three rules I promised myself I'd always keep."

Her eyelids fluttered open, and she met his gaze.

"Rule number one." He traced her mouth with the pad of his thumb. "Don't date employees."

"Rule number two." He cut her off when she opened her mouth. "Hotel policies apply to the entire staff."

"Sam—"

"Rule number three." He placed his index finger on her lips. "Don't get emotionally involved with an employee."

When she parted her lips, heat slammed into his gut. "I've known you less than two weeks," he said, "and I've already broken every damn one."

"You know," she whispered, "since I'm no longer an employee, those rules don't really apply anymore, do they?"

"No, I suppose they don't," he said, then grabbed hold of her shoulders and dragged her mouth to his.

Seven

Crazy.

Unbelievably, undeniably, wondrously crazy.

His mouth on hers, his arms crushing her against him, drove every rational thought from her mind. She didn't want to think, and how could she, with her heart thundering in her head the way it was?

She was too damn tired to fight her emotions any longer. She wanted, *needed,* as she never had before. When his lips moved to her ear, she rolled her head back on a soft moan.

Pressing closer to him, she wrapped her arms around his neck, felt giddy with the excitement rushing through her. But somewhere, far away, on the edges of her mind, she heard a tiny voice. *Are you insane? You're in the hotel. The entire kitchen staff watched you leave with Sam!*

"Sam," she managed a weak protest. "This is—"

"I know." He nipped at her earlobe.

She shivered violently. "We shouldn't—"

"No," he agreed, and blazed kisses down her neck.

There, right there, she thought when his mouth nuzzled the base of her throat. "Someone might—"

"They might."

She sucked in a breath when his teeth sank into her skin. "Will you stop being so damn agreeable?"

"Okay," he murmured.

His mouth caught hers again, kissed her long and hard. A hot, wild meeting of tongue and teeth and lips. Her pulse raced; heat swept through her veins like a firestorm, turning her insides to liquid. Certain her bones were melting, she clung to him, afraid she might slide to the floor.

But the carpet *was* soft, she thought dimly. Soft and cushioned.

And so close…

So decadent…

She arched up into him, felt the full length of his solid body against hers, the hard press of his erection. Her breasts tingled with anticipation, her skin tightened, and the intensity of the sensations might have been painful if she hadn't been so completely and utterly aroused.

Her fingers hurried up his neck, curled into his thick, smooth hair. The texture shivered from her fingertips all the way down to her toes. She breathed in the scent of his skin, a heady mix of pure male and hot passion, then rushed her hands down again, slid under the lapels of his suit jacket and slid it off his broad shoulders.

Through the rolling haze of desire, she felt him backing her across the room. Toward the sofa? she wondered. The bedroom? It didn't matter, just as long as they got there *soon*. As long as he never stopped kissing her.

She fumbled with the knot of his tie, cursed her inability to make her fingers work faster. Finally, with a *whoosh* of silk, the tie slid from her hand and dropped soundlessly to the floor. She worked at the top button of his shirt, felt his low growl against her fingertips when she opened buttons and slid her hands inside. The feel of his muscled chest under her palms, the heat of his skin, sent ripples of white-hot need coursing through her.

So it *was* the bedroom he was directing her toward, she realized when she bumped into the doorjamb. She opened her eyes just enough to catch a glimpse of smoke-colored walls, a mahogany armoire and late afternoon sunlight streaming through the open, dark blue drapes. She couldn't see the bed from this angle, but she knew it was there, and the thought of making love with Sam, of having him inside her, made her shudder fiercely.

His kisses swept like liquid fire across her jaw, over her chin, down her neck. Certain she couldn't take any more, she raked her fingernails down his chest, moved her hands toward the buckle of his belt.

"Sam…" She heard the desperation in her voice, his ragged breathing, her heart slamming against her ribs. The sounds swirled in her head, melded together. She kicked her flats off, then rose on the tips of her toes and wantonly moved her hips against him.

On a groan, he tugged her blouse from her slacks

and slid his hands underneath, rushed his fingers over her rib cage.

"So damn soft," he murmured.

As if in slow motion, she felt herself falling backward onto the mattress, the descent steep and long and exciting. His hands covered her breasts, and she sank into a river of erotic sensations, let herself be swept away in the swirling waters.

"I've been crazy wanting this," he said huskily. "Wanting you."

Crazy. There it was again. The word that seemed to say it all. She looked at Sam, saw the fierce desire glinting in his narrowed eyes as he stared down at her. Crazy or not, how could something that felt this right be wrong?

When he lowered his head to her bare stomach, she simply didn't care anymore.

It surprised Sam how fragile Kiera felt under him. She was tall for a woman, but her bone structure was delicate, her curves soft and smooth, her breasts firm and round. Her fingers moved restlessly over his back when he touched his lips to the hollow of her belly. When he swept his tongue over her warm, silky skin, she squirmed under him.

The sweet taste of her nearly sent him over the edge, but he held back, wanting, needing to draw that sweetness out. He nipped at the edge of her rib cage, heard her sharp intake of breath. She arched upward, and he slid his hands underneath her, unclasped her bra and shoved the lacy garment up.

When he took one hardened nipple in his mouth, she gasped and raked her fingers over his scalp. He suckled one breast, then the other, teased the peak of each nipple with his tongue and his teeth. The need he felt for her rocked him to the core. *Slow it down,* he told himself. *Get yourself back in control, dammit.*

Then she moved her hips against him and whispered his name.

Oh, to hell with it.

Flipping open the single button on her slacks, he blazed kisses along the underside of her breast while he tugged the zipper down, then slid his hand inside to cup her. Soft lace pressed against his palm. When he tightened his grip, she groaned.

Every breath burned his lungs, sweat beaded on his forehead. If he wasn't inside her soon, he thought he might go mad.

He slid between lace and skin and slipped a finger into the wet heat between her thighs. She bucked upward, and when he stroked her, he felt the bite of her nails across his shoulders.

"Take…off…your…clothes," she gasped and hurried her hands to his belt buckle.

He brushed her hands away, knew he didn't dare let her touch him yet. "You first."

In one fluid sweep of his hands, he had her slacks and underwear off and tossed them aside. She rose up, managed to undo the knot on her own tie and yank it off, then reached for him. But he moved too quickly, tugged her blouse downward, pinning her arms and dragging her closer while he dropped his mouth down on hers.

She couldn't move, could barely breathe, and she thought she might die if he didn't hurry. Heat coursed through her, coiled between her legs. She wanted desperately to touch him, but he'd trapped her arms, frustrating her. Exciting her. Thrilling her as no man ever had before.

"I can't stand it," she said raggedly, dropping her head back when his mouth moved to her neck. He sucked lightly, then used his teeth. Flames raced over her skin. "Sam, *please*."

Hopelessly and wonderfully lost in the sensations battering her, she couldn't think, could only *feel* as he moved over her with his mouth and teeth and tongue. She trembled with need, wantonly arched upward, frantic for him to be inside her.

When he released her arms, she fell backward and lay naked under him. He unbuckled his belt and unzipped his pants. She drew in a breath when he shoved his pants and black boxers down. He was hard and fully erect.

And large.

Her eyes widened, and she felt a moment's apprehension. He slid his hands up her legs, her thighs, his gaze dark and fierce and primal. He spread her legs and she gripped the bedclothes as he moved over her.

He entered her, moving deeper with each thrust, then deeper still, until he was fully sheathed inside her. She released the breath she'd been holding and wrapped her arms and legs around him, felt the rippling sinew under her limbs.

And then he began to move.

Slowly at first, his rhythm building gradually. Exquisitely. Moaning, she clung to him, every thrust of his hips coiling the pleasure inside her tighter, then tighter still. Blood pounded in her temples, raced through her veins, until she burst apart.

She cried out, bit her lip as the shudders tore through her like shards of colored glass. When he groaned and thrust deeper, harder, she held him tight, felt his muscles bunch under her hands. He moaned, deep in his throat, then his body convulsed with his release.

He collapsed on top of her, pressing her into the mattress. Closing her eyes, she slid her arms around his neck and smiled.

It took a few moments for Sam to regain any sort of order to his brain. With his breathing still ragged, he rolled to his back, bringing Kiera with him. She lay over him like a rag doll, her head on his shoulder, her warm, soft breath fanning his chest. A fine sheen of sweat covered their bodies.

Reality slowly came back. They were in his bedroom, on his bed, their clothes tossed on the floor. He could still hear his blood pounding in his temples, though not quite as loudly as a few minutes ago.

He stilled when he saw the impressions on her arms left by his hands.

"Dammit," he said through clenched teeth. "Did I hurt you?"

"Hurt me?" she mumbled without moving.

"I was a little rough." He felt like an idiot, losing control like that with her. "I should have been more careful."

"Did I act like I wanted careful?" She slid her hand up his chest.

Gently, he traced a fingertip over the marks on her arms. "You may have a bruise or two."

She raised her head and rested her chin on her hand, gave him a sultry smile. "You may have a few yourself, mister. Maybe *I* should have been more careful with you."

He grinned at her. "Bring it on, darlin'."

"I love a challenge." She slid her hand down his chest, then his belly. Her smile turned wicked. "You may live to regret those words."

He hadn't a chance to answer, couldn't have come up with anything witty even if she *had* given him a chance. But the second her hand closed over him, his brain locked up and his body took over. When she brushed her lips across his stomach, he sucked in a breath through clenched teeth.

"I see we're off to a good start," she murmured, touching her tongue to his skin.

He couldn't have agreed with her more.

When he woke, the room was dark, the bed beside him empty. His brain was thick as mud, his throat dry and coarse. He rose on one elbow and winced, realized he must have pulled a muscle in his bad shoulder.

But at least he was alive.

Barely.

Frowning, he sat, scrubbed a hand over his face, then shook the cobwebs from his brain and waited for his eyes to adjust to the dark. He glanced at the bedside clock: 8:57. He swore, irritated that he'd lost over an hour sleeping.

And given Kiera an opportunity to escape without an argument.

Any other woman, any other time, he wouldn't have been annoyed. Hell, it had always been easier if he'd been alone when he woke up. Usually, after he made love to a woman he didn't have a great deal to say, and he sure didn't want to deal with the emotional expectations some women built up in their minds.

But this wasn't any other time, and this sure as hell wasn't any other woman. Without question, Kiera was one of a kind. Sexy, funny, confident, and yet strangely innocent at the same time. He'd never met anyone like her in his life. He rotated his shoulder, preferring the sharp pain of a tweaked muscle to the strange, dull ache in his chest.

Tossing the bedcovers off, he sat on the edge of the mattress, spotted his slacks at the foot of the bed, had barely yanked them on when he stilled. The amazing smell of warm chocolate wafted in from the other room. His first thought was one of relief that she hadn't left, but then he frowned, couldn't imagine that under the circumstances she had ordered room service.

Dragging a hand through his hair, he moved to the bedroom door, felt his heart slam against his ribs when he caught sight of her.

She stood in the kitchen, wearing nothing but his shirt. She hummed softly, her arms elbow-deep in dish soap bubbles. He leaned against the doorjamb, took in the endless length of sleek legs, the curve of her bottom, her shiny black hair tumbling down, resting on her shoulders. How could he want her again

so soon? he wondered. They'd fallen into bed nearly an hour ago, and all he could think about was dragging her back.

But he wouldn't. Not yet, anyway. At some masculine level, he felt a profound sense of satisfaction simply watching her. He glanced at the oven, couldn't imagine what she was baking in there, especially considering how little food he kept stocked in his cupboards. But if there was a kitchen in heaven, he thought he'd just stepped into it, complete with his own gorgeous angel.

He pushed away from the doorjamb and moved toward her. "Smells good."

She glanced over her shoulder at him, smiled. "Wait till you taste it."

He came up behind her, brushed her hair aside and kissed her neck. "I can't wait."

"I'm busy here, buster." But she leaned back against him with a sigh.

"I'm busy, too." He nipped her neck with his teeth, felt the shiver move through her. "Don't mind me, you just keep doing whatever it is you're doing."

"I'm washing the bowls and utensils I used." She'd tried to sound impatient, but her tone was more seductive than clipped.

"Used for what?" he asked, but he was much more interested in that little spot behind her ear that made her breath catch.

"I felt like baking." She wasn't even pretending to wash dishes anymore. Eyes closed, she'd tilted her head back and laid it on his shoulder.

"What do you feel like now?" He nibbled on her

earlobe, then slid his hands under the hem of her shirt, traced the curve of her hips with his palms.

The steady, high-pitched *beep, beep, beep* of a timer rudely interrupted.

Damn.

Straightening, Kiera shook her arms free of bubbles, grabbed a towel sitting on the counter and moved to the oven. He watched her open the door and pull out a tray holding two coffee mugs.

His irritation at being interrupted shifted to amazement. A steaming dome of chocolate bubbled around the rim of the coffee mugs.

"I hope you like soufflé," she said, setting the tray on the stove top.

Soufflé? He furrowed his brow. She'd made *soufflé?*

"You don't have much in your cupboards or refrigerator." She bit her lip. "But I found a few eggs, some sugar packets and pats of butter. I had the chocolate bar in my purse."

He stared at the coffee cups in disbelief, still trying to absorb the fact that she'd actually made soufflé.

"It's better hot." She picked up a spoon from the counter and handed it to him. He scooped out a bite of the dessert and tried it, felt an explosion of chocolate pleasure on his tongue.

Good Lord. Too stunned to speak, he simply stared at her.

"I realize I should have left," she rushed on, twisting the towel in her hands. "But it's still a little early and I was worried someone might see me."

"You baked this," he finally managed. "In my kitchen."

She shifted uneasily. "I hope you don't mind."

"Mind?" He stepped closer to her, tugged the towel from her hands and tossed it on the counter. "A half-naked, sexy woman makes me the best damn chocolate soufflé I've had in my entire life and you think I would mind?"

He pulled her into his arms, caught her small gasp with his mouth and kissed her. Not with the desperate hunger clawing unexpectedly in his gut, but softly, so softly he surprised himself. Her lips parted, warm and willing, her eyes fluttered closed.

"This is how much I mind," he murmured against her mouth, felt her smile. "Miss Daniels, you are the damnedest woman."

She stilled, then laid her palms on his chest and eased back, kept her gaze lowered. "Sam—" she paused "—Daniels isn't exactly my last name."

He could have told her he already knew she'd lied about that. He'd looked at her file the first day she'd been hired, and he'd also ran a search on her name. He'd found nothing that came close to matching any information she'd given on her application or even anything she'd told him. Except that Rainville, Texas, was famous for its bee festival.

He could have—*should* have—had her fired. Still wasn't sure why he hadn't. But he'd simply trusted his gut and looked the other way.

Standing in his kitchen, holding her, he could feel her internal struggle with revealing even this small piece of truth. As badly as he wanted to, he knew if he pushed her she might disappear as quickly as she'd shown up.

And if he knew anything at all, he knew he wanted her to stay.

"I'm sorry I lied," she said quietly. "But I needed this job."

He felt the cool slide of cotton when he ran his palms up her arms. "You're rehired."

"I can't stay, Sam." With a sigh, she dropped her hands to her sides. "Chef Phillipe—"

"I'll handle Phillipe."

Shaking her head, she stepped away. "It's better this way."

"Better?" He narrowed his eyes. "Better for whom?"

"For everyone," she insisted. "The restaurant, the staff, the hotel. For you."

He reached out and snagged her arms, pulled her close again. "Don't tell me what's better for me. What the hell were we doing here today?"

Blue fire sparked in her eyes. "What are you saying, that you think I slept with you so I could keep my job?"

"Of course not." Hell, he didn't know what he was saying. His hands tightened on her arms, but he could feel her slipping away. "Dammit, Kiera, if you run away every time there's a problem—"

"Let go of me." The fire in her eyes turned to ice. "Now."

Swearing, he let go of her, watched her chin lift as she stepped back.

"You don't know anything about me," she said, shaking her head. "Nothing."

"That's the understatement of the century." He hadn't intended to sound sarcastic, but that damn stubborn streak of hers had put a crack in his hard-won patience.

Narrowing her eyes, she turned and walked toward the bedroom.

"Dammit, Kiera," he yelled after her. "Where do you think you're going?"

"I'm leaving." She shot him a cool glance over her shoulder. "Don't worry, I'll take the suite elevator down so no one will see me."

"Did I say I was worried?" he snapped, clenching his jaw when she disappeared into the bedroom.

He started after her, swore, then stopped, raked a hand through his hair. Swore again.

No woman had ever made him feel helpless like this before. Made him feel out of control or cut off at the knees. He didn't like it.

Not one damn bit.

He wouldn't chase after her. If she wanted to leave, he told himself, then fine. She could leave. If she wanted to be so damn secretive, then that was fine, too.

He couldn't keep her here against her will—well, actually, he probably could—but he didn't want her that way. He wanted her to trust him. He wanted her honesty. She wasn't willing to give him either one.

So when she came back out of the bedroom, her head high and shoulders squared, he let her leave, made no attempt to stop her.

Long after she was gone, the taste of her, a sweet mix of chocolate and woman, lingered in his mouth. He drowned it with a bottle of scotch and cursed the day she'd walked into his hotel.

Eight

Kiera yanked open the dresser drawer, grabbed a pair of jeans and threw them in her suitcase. Three tank tops followed, along with an assortment of bras and panties. She stormed across the bedroom into the bathroom, picked up her pink-striped toiletry case, then stomped back and tossed that in the suitcase, as well.

Sam Prescott had to be the most impossible, difficult she'd ever met. To think that she'd actually *slept* with the man infuriated her. She'd heard every warning bell, spotted every Off Limits sign, and yet she'd completely ignored every one of them. She'd let muscles, a smooth tongue and a pretty face override logic and sweep her off her feet.

She paused and stared at herself in the mirror, then sighed in disgust. Given the chance, she knew she'd do it all over again.

In a heartbeat, dammit.

She'd spent half of last night berating herself for sleeping with Sam, the other half wishing she was still in his bed. It grated on her pride that she'd so easily, and eagerly, gone to his bed.

She picked up a brush and pointed it at her reflection. "Couldn't you have shown even a little hesitation?" she said with exasperation. "Did you have to throw yourself at him?"

Turning away, she dropped the brush into the hanging travel bag on the back of the bathroom door, then closed the zipper. When she looked back in the mirror, it wasn't her own face she saw, but Sam's.

Dammit, Kiera, if you run away every time there's a problem...

"I'm not running away from anything," she snapped at the mirror, then spun on her heels and walked back into the bedroom. Her packed suitcase laying open on the bed screamed that she was a liar.

Okay, so maybe this time she *was* running away. But sleeping with Sam had exacerbated an already complicated situation. If she stayed, the situation could only get worse.

If she stayed, she'd fall in love.

Oh, who are you kidding? she thought, then sank down on the edge of the bed. What was the use in denying it?

She'd already fallen in love.

Hard.

She cursed herself, then Sam. She didn't want to be in love. Not this kind of love; the ache-in-the-chest, weak-kneed, I-want-to-have-your-babies-can't-live-without-you kind of love. She'd seen what that kind of love had done to her mother, how it had destroyed her. Until Sam, she hadn't understood feelings like that, hadn't understood how a man could have the power to take away a woman's self-respect, her identity. But last night, when she'd left Sam's suite the overwhelming urge to run back to him, to give him anything in the world he asked for, scared the hell out of her.

That was why she had to leave Wolf River. To prove to herself she wasn't so far gone that she couldn't walk away. So far gone that she couldn't, in time, forget about him and love someone else.

She'd hadn't come here to fall in love. She'd come for answers to questions. She'd come to find out the truth behind the lie. But here she was, questions still unanswered, the truth still beyond her reach, her heart aching.

Part of her wanted to go home to Stone Ridge Ranch. She knew she'd find comfort there, knew that Alaina would soothe her pain, that Alexis would call from New York and give her a pep talk and tell her there were dozens of good-looking men, why fuss over one? Even Trey, who would undoubtedly yell for an hour or two, would soften when he saw she was hurting. Then he'd probably go and beat Sam up.

The thought actually lightened her mood for a moment, but she knew, of course, that she couldn't go home. Not now. Not for a long time.

So Paris it was, she'd decided, even though the initial excitement over her trip was now nonexistent. Paris would give her a chance to regroup, to refocus and let her heart mend.

She jolted at the sound of the knock from the other room. *Sam!* She quickly tamped down the urge to jump up and sprint across the room. Instead, she slowly drew in a deep, calming breath and waited for a second knock. *Let him stew,* she thought, pleased with herself that she strolled, not ran, across the living room.

But it wasn't Sam standing there, Kiera discovered when she opened the door.

It was Clair.

The spark of cool indifference she'd worked up to greet Sam fizzled, then sputtered out. "Clair, hello."

Clair, dressed neatly in a chic, navy-blue pantsuit, had more color in her face today, and a firm sense of purpose that made Kiera uneasy.

"May I come in?" she asked.

"Of course." Kiera stepped aside, couldn't help but notice the somber tone in Clair's voice. "Is something wrong?"

"Yes, actually, something is wrong." Clair moved inside and glanced toward the sofa. "May I sit down?"

"Of course." Worried, Kiera closed the door behind her and followed her into the living room. *The baby,* was her first thought, and she felt the panic twist in her stomach. *Or Sam.* Something had happened to Sam!

No, that didn't make any sense. Even if something had happened to Sam, Clair wouldn't have come here. She didn't know about yesterday, Kiera thought. No one knew that she and Sam, well, that they'd been together. In his suite. Intimately.

Or did they?

Her stomach clenched even tighter at the thought,

and she searched her brain for some kind of explanation. Not that there was one, she realized. She and Sam had slept together. That hardly required an explanation. Biting her lip, she watched Clair sit on the sofa, her back straight as a pin, her gaze no-nonsense.

"I understand you quit yesterday."

Speechless, Kiera stared at Clair in amazement. *That's* why she'd come here? Kiera realized that Clair was a hands-on owner, but still, one waitress quitting hardly warranted a personal visit.

"I—I'm sorry." Her brain still stumbling over Clair's statement, Kiera had to clear her throat before she could speak again. "I assure you, normally I would have given two weeks' notice, but under the circumstances it seemed like the best thing to do."

"The circumstances," Clair repeated thoughtfully. Her dark hair brushed one shoulder when she tilted her head. "Are you referring to Phillipe's temper tantrum or your relationship with Sam?"

Kiera's breath caught. *Sam had told Clair?* Anger slowly seeped through her shock. How *could* he!

"I can see what you're thinking." Clair shook her head. "And you can relax. Sam didn't say a word to me, about you quitting or anything else. He's hardly the type of man to kiss and tell."

Relief swept through Kiera, along with a blush. "But—"

"I'm not blind, Kiera," Clair said with a soft smile. "I saw the way he looked at you that afternoon in my office. In all the time I've known him, I've never seen him look at any woman like that. Do you know he handed me a letter of resignation this morning?"

Kiera sank down on the sofa beside Clair. "He did *what?*"

"I told him I wouldn't accept it unless he'd murdered a guest, and even then I might take into consideration whom he'd killed. There's an oafish brute on the fourth floor driving the entire staff crazy."

It took Kiera a moment to realize Clair was making a joke. "He—Sam—" She could feel her pulse throbbing in her temple. "Did he say why?"

"Just that his contract was up and he thought it was time for him to leave," Clair said. "Then I heard you called in this morning and quit, so I knew something was going on. It didn't take long for me to find out about the fracas in the kitchen yesterday with Phillipe, then put together the pieces from there."

This isn't happening, Kiera thought desperately, wishing she would just wake up from this bad dream. She'd intentionally antagonized Phillipe, slept with her boss, then quit her job and Clair knew everything. And if that wasn't bad enough, Sam had quit, too.

Kiera couldn't imagine what this woman thought of her. Wasn't even certain what she thought of herself, for that matter. "Clair, I'm sorry," Kiera said hoarsely. "I—"

"Stop right there." Clair shook her head. "I did not come here for an apology. Whatever did or didn't happen between you and Sam yesterday doesn't concern me. What does concern me is the prosperity of the Four Winds. Sam has increased business thirty percent since he came to work for me and I don't want to lose him. But even more important to me..." she added, her voice softening "...he's my friend, a good friend. I don't want to lose that, either."

"But you refused his resignation." If she was the reason that Sam left the Four Winds, Kiera could never forgive herself. "He's going to stay, isn't he?"

"I hope so," Clair said, then covered Kiera's hand with her own. "But it's not just Sam I don't want to lose, Kiera. I don't want to lose you, either. If you're worried about Phillipe, you needn't be. He'll be gone in two weeks."

"Gone?" Kiera swallowed hard. "Surely not because of anything that I—"

"No, no, no." Clair laughed softly. "There have been problems from the first day we hired him, and we overlooked them because he had the credentials and a six-month contract. I'd hoped we could weather it out until Chef Bartollini returned, but we found out he's not coming back. Sam and I agreed it wasn't a good idea to tell Phillipe we've hired a replacement."

"You've hired a new chef?" Just the thought improved Kiera's dark mood, but then she realized that Sam had known yesterday. She'd ranted and raved about Phillipe and what an idiot the man was, and Sam hadn't said a word about a new chef!

"As much as I want Phillipe gone," Clair continued, "if he quits before the new chef can start, I may have to close the restaurant. Between the Cattlemen's conference this next week and the Central Texas Retailer's Association coming the week after, we'll be in big trouble. One little coffee shop couldn't possibly handle the needs of that many guests."

It would be a nightmare if they had to close Adagio's even for a day, Kiera realized. Between the complaints and the lost revenue, the Four Winds would feel the bite big-time.

"Tell me what I can do to convince you to stay at Adagio's," Clair said, squeezing Kiera's hand. "More money? Better hours? A promotion? Just name it."

Clair's generosity, and her kindness, only increased Kiera's guilt. *Tell her,* her conscience whispered. *Tell her who you are, why you came. You owe her the truth. Tell her now...*

But she couldn't. Coward that she was, she couldn't bear to lose Clair's trust.

"I'm flattered, truly I am." She slipped her hand from Clair's. "But I'm not just leaving the restaurant, I'm leaving Wolf River."

"You're leaving Wolf River?" Disappointment and surprise lined Clair's brow. "Because of Sam?"

"It's more complicated than that." More than she could ever explain. "Thank you, but I'm sorry, I can't stay."

Clair shook her head and sighed. "And I was so hoping you could be there."

Kiera frowned. "Be where?"

"At my cousin Dillon's Fourth of July barbecue. Jacob and I are going to announce we're pregnant." Her eyes sparkling, Clair grabbed both of Kiera's hands. "It's only a week away. I can see you're determined to leave, but please, just stay a little longer and come to Dillon's. I'd love for you to meet my family, be there when we tell everyone the good news."

"You want me—" Kiera swallowed hard "—to meet your family?"

"You'll love them," Clair said enthusiastically. "And the Blackhawk Ranch is absolutely amazing."

The Blackhawk Ranch? Kiera's heart raced, and she had to pull her hands away from Clair before she could see how badly they were shaking. "But, but, I couldn't—"

Unswayed, and obviously delighted with her plan, Clair scooped up her purse from the sofa and slipped it over her shoulder. "Of course you can. Now promise me you'll come and I promise I won't make you feel guilty over quitting, which was my last ace to play, by the way." The Blackhawk Ranch, Kiera thought dimly. The Blackhawk family. *Dillon Blackhawk.* Panic ripped through her, took her breath away. Dear God. She couldn't. She *couldn't.*

But she had to, she realized. It was her one opportunity, her last opportunity to find out who these people were. To find out who *she* was.

"Practically half the town is coming," Clair said, then, as if to sweeten the deal, added, "Sam will be there, too."

Kiera wasn't certain if that was a good thing or not, but the thought of seeing him again, even if just one last time, made her heart beat all the faster.

"All right." Kiera sucked in a deep breath, prayed she wasn't making a mistake. "I'll come."

The reservations desk and lobby of the Four Winds was crowded with early check-ins for the upcoming Cattlemen's conference. The event was scheduled to open July fifth, but quite a few of the attendees came in before the first day for the "Shoot the Bull" sessions where the ranchers talked shop in a less structured environment that included plenty of alcohol, cigars, food and more than one friendly game of late night cards. Ranchers worked hard and played hard, and the Four Winds welcomed their business.

Sam stood on the sidelines, watched closely to ensure that each guest was greeted with a smile, offered drinks and cookies while they waited in line to register and reminded them that the hotel spa was taking reservations for massage and facial packages. Like a well-oiled machine, every employee did their job smoothly and efficiently—exactly as they'd been trained.

He studied the flow of cars being valeted, the stream of people moving through the double glass doors, and it gave him satisfaction to know that even in the flurry of activity surrounding him, there was a controlled system operating. Order in chaos, he thought.

Which pretty much summed up his own life, he decided. Only without the order part.

It irritated the hell out of him that Kiera had actually quit, that she wouldn't even discuss letting him handle the situation with Phillipe. If she'd have given him a chance, he might have even told her that Phillipe would be gone in two weeks.

But she hadn't given him a chance, he thought, clenching his jaw. She'd simply walked out without so much as a backward glance.

The damn woman made him crazy.

No woman had ever driven him crazy before. No woman had ever got under his skin the way Kiera had.

He hadn't even been able to sleep in his own bed last night. He'd smelled the scent of her shampoo on his pillow, seen her lying there on his bed, her hair flowing like a black river, her eyes glazed with passion, heard her whispering his name.

He'd had to sleep on the sofa, though he'd hardly call lying there most of the night, angry one minute, worried the next, sleeping. But somewhere during the night, just before the sky began to lighten with the new day, he'd decided he wasn't giving her the easy way out. That he wasn't letting her walk away. If she wanted a fight, fine.

He'd give her a fight.

He decided he'd give her a day or two to calm down and think things over before he had it out with her. He'd also decided that it was probably best that she had quit. He couldn't, in good conscience, have a personal relationship with her if she worked here, and he sure as hell had no intention of sneaking around. As it was, he'd already destroyed his integrity as general manager.

Even though Kiera had quit, he still felt he'd had no choice but to hand Clair his resignation. His blatant breach of policy had demanded he resign. He would have expected nothing less from any other employee in a management position. As general manager, he had a duty to the hotel, to Clair and to all the employees.

But Clair had firmly refused his resignation, had insisted he couldn't possibly leave with two conferences coming in back to back, and who else could handle Phillipe when he was given his walking papers? Though he'd been determined when he walked into her office, Clair had served a sufficient dose of guilt to change his mind.

For the time being, at least, he'd stay.

"Excuse me, mister, but can you tell me where I might find the manager of this joint?"

Sam glanced over his shoulder. Clair stood beside him, a worried look in her eyes. "Is there a problem, miss?"

"A big problem. See, there's this scary guy hanging around the lobby who looks like he wants to hurt someone, and I thought maybe you could ask him to leave."

Concerned, Sam quickly scanned the room, then realized he'd been had. Lifting an eyebrow, he looked back at Clair. "What does this guy look like?"

"Well, I'll be darned." She leaned in close and squinted her eyes. "He looks just like you."

"All right, all right," he said with a sigh, then relaxed his shoulders and even managed a grin. Given his state of mind, he supposed he might have looked less than approachable. "I get your point."

"Can't have you frightening small children and fainthearted women," Clair said cheerfully, then added, "Come have lunch with me."

"I should probably keep an eye on check-ins." He glanced back at the crowd, happily sipping water and champagne and munching on chocolate cookies.

"You know perfectly well our staff can handle check-ins." Clair slipped an arm though his. "I'm starving. Have lunch with me and I'll tell you about my visit with Kiera this morning."

He froze, then looked down at Clair. "What about Kiera?"

"I figured that would get your attention," she said, looking much too pleased with herself. "Come on,

I'm starving. Jacob's gone to pick Evan and Marcy up from the airport and I don't want to eat alone. We'll talk over lunch."

"We're here, Miss Daniels."

Busy chewing on the ragged edge of a fingernail— a bad habit she'd determinedly kicked twelve years ago—Kiera hadn't realized the car had stopped. She'd held her paper-thin nerves together by reciting recipes and converting ingredient measurements in her head, a practice she'd picked up from her childhood days spent with Cookie in the kitchen. But all the measurement conversions and nail biting in the world couldn't stop the sudden nausea rolling through her stomach.

She was at the Blackhawk Ranch.

"Are you all right?" The limousine driver glanced at her in his rearview mirror. He had friendly eyes, a thick, salt-and-pepper mustache and eyebrows to match.

"Thank you, I'm fine." Kiera smiled weakly at the man. Clair had called three minutes before the car and chauffeur had shown up, and though Kiera had insisted she could drive herself, Clair had refused to take no for an answer. The driver, Martin, had entertained her with stories of Wolf River residents, including the three teen-agers who'd thrown a firecracker down what they thought was a gopher hole, but was really an air vent for their daddy's underground moonshine shed. "Blew a hole in the backyard the size of a tractor," Martin had told her. "Fortunately for the boys, their daddy hadn't been in there at the time."

The driver handed her a card with his cell phone

number. "I'll be going back and forth from town until midnight. Just call me when you're ready to go home."

How about right now? she thought, but simply thanked him and took the card, then took a deep breath and stepped out of the shiny white limousine. Groups of people streamed past her while trucks and cars maneuvered for parking spots. Children, boys and girls, ran in circles around two small barking balls of fur. Music floated on the air, along with the enticing scent of grilling meat.

Kiera stood amid the flurry of activity, felt the breeze lift the hem of her long denim dress. When the limousine drove away, gravel crunching under its tires, it took a will of iron not to turn and run after it.

I don't belong here, she told herself. She could call Martin right now, before he even made it back to the highway, and she could leave.

And then she saw the house.

It towered two stories high, redbrick with white trim and two sets of wide bay windows. Dormers winked grandly across the slate-gray roof, and tall, double oak entry doors flanked by bouncing red, white and blue balloons greeted guests. Beyond the house stretched acre after acre of low rolling hills and thick-branched oak trees.

The house drew her, and she moved with the flow of people, down a flagstone walkway past a tidy bed of yellow daisies and white petunias, up the porch steps, then through the gleaming double doors. Inside, the house was even more magnificent. White marbled entry and sweeping staircase. White walls with a high ceiling and crystal chandelier.

Certainly not like any ranch house she'd ever seen before. And definitely not like the one she'd been raised in.

The interior of the house might have been considered cold if not for the festive red, white and blue streamers and balloons decorating the staircase and the three-foot floral display on an entry table. When the children who'd been playing outside streaked through the front door, shrieking and screaming like little banshees, Kiera stepped out of the way into a narrow hallway under the stairs. She watched them, couldn't help but wonder how her life might have been different if she'd been raised here instead of Stone Ridge. Would she think differently? Act differently? Want different things?

From the corner of her eye, she spotted the framed photographs on the wall. Family photos, she realized, including the same one that Clair had in her office with herself and her brothers. There were several more, but one that caught her eye and made her pulse jump—a man with his arms around a pretty redhead. The distant sound of a band tuning up and the din of voices faded away. Breath held, she leaned in closer, saw the unmistakable Blackhawk features. She knew in her heart this was Dillon Blackhawk, which made him William Blackhawk's son.

The thought sent a chill up her spine. She searched frantically for a photo of the man, but strangely, there were none. When her mother had lived at Stone Ridge, she'd enshrined William Blackhawk's image with candles and crucifixes. Here, there was nothing.

"Hey."

Kiera jumped at the sound of the man's voice and spun around, hand clutching her throat.

Sam.

The black cowboy hat surprised her, but it suited him, she decided. She drank in the sight of him, appreciated the way his navy-blue Western shirt accentuated his broad shoulders. His jeans, slightly worn and low on his hips, showed off his long, powerful legs. It was all she could do not to slip a finger under his silver embossed belt buckle and pull him closer. "You scared me."

"I know." Unsmiling, his eyes burned into hers. "Sorry 'bout that. I'll be more careful."

She had the distinct feeling he wasn't talking about now, but the other night. She hadn't seen him since they'd made love, and she'd missed him, had struggled with wishing he would call and hoping he wouldn't.

But now, looking into his dark brown eyes, breathing in the now familiar scent of his skin, the past week and her irritation melted away. She couldn't even remember why she'd walked out, why she'd wasted one precious minute of the short time they would have together. Desperately she wanted to throw herself in his arms, might have if the procession of guests moving through the house hadn't suddenly seemed to increase. But here, standing in this hallway under the stairs, it seemed as if she and Sam were the only two people in the world.

"You hiding out here?" he asked.

"Maybe a little," she admitted. "I thought maybe if I looked at some of the photos, I'd at least recognize a few people here today, even if I don't know their names."

Sam glanced at the wall, studied the pictures for a

moment. "You saw this one with Clair and her brothers, Rand and Seth, and this one—" he pointed at a large group picture "—looks like the entire Blackhawk family."

Not the entire Blackhawk family, Kiera thought, clutching the strap of her purse. "There are so many of them."

"Growing bigger every day," he said with a nod. "I could name them, or just take you outside and introduce you. Everyone's here."

Everyone's here. Her heart beat faster at the thought. Was she walking into quicksand? She was certain if Sam weren't here, she would call the limo driver right now and ask him to come get her.

But Sam was here, and his presence gave her the courage she needed to see this through. "I think I just need a minute."

"Okay." He leaned back against the wall, and slowly swept his eyes over her. "Nice dress."

Her blood warmed under his perusal; her skin tingled. When his gaze reached her feet, he lifted a surprised brow and glanced back up.

"Nice boots, too."

"Thanks." She'd bought the brown leather cowboy boots in town yesterday, even though she already had a closet full at her family's ranch. She glanced at Sam's polished black boots and smiled. "I like yours, too."

"They're required wear at Texas barbecues." He pushed away from the wall and closed the space between them. "Especially for a two-step."

She arched an eyebrow. "The boss man dances?"

"With you, I do." He ran a fingertip along her shoulder. "And I'm not your boss, anymore. Remember?"

"I remember." She shivered at his touch. She remembered everything. "So, are you any good?"

He lifted one corner of his mouth in a slow grin.

"At dancing," she added, held her breath when his fingertip moved to her collarbone.

"Damn good," he said with a nod. "So is that a yes?"

What woman could say no to this man? she wondered. *Obviously, not me.* The light touch of his fingertip tracing the edge of her neckline curled her toes. "It's a maybe."

"I'll accept that for now." He slid his hand down her arm. "I missed you, Kiera."

She dropped her gaze, watched him lace his fingers with hers, felt her heart swell. "I missed you, too."

"I've been worried about you, had to call Mattie every day to make sure you were all right."

Surprised, she looked up. "You called Mattie? At the Shangri-La?"

"I didn't think you wanted to talk to me," he said, squeezing her hand. "Mattie always wants to talk."

Wasn't that the truth? Kiera thought with a soft laugh. She told herself she should be mad at Sam for checking up on her, or maybe just because he hadn't called her himself. And maybe later she would be mad at him. But not now, she decided. Not today.

Today she wanted to simply enjoy being with him. To enjoy dancing with him. Today she wouldn't worry about tomorrow. Today she would live for the moment.

And tonight…

"Excuse me."

A man's voice from behind Sam had Kiera pulling

her hand away. When she looked up, all thoughts of enjoying herself shattered.

Dillon Blackhawk stood in the hallway. He smiled hesitantly when her gaze met his.

"Sorry to interrupt," Dillon said, then turned his attention to Sam. "But I've been sent to find you."

Nine

If Sam hadn't been touching Kiera when Dillon spoke, he might not have noticed anything strange except for the brief widening of her eyes and terse intake of breath. A normal reaction for anyone who'd been surprised.

But in that brief second before she'd pulled her hand from his, he'd felt something ripple through Kiera when she'd looked into Dillon's eyes. Panic, he thought, and recognition—an awareness, of sorts, that went far beyond the ordinary.

"Just got here." Sam turned to Dillon and shook the man's hand. "How's it going?"

"Can't complain." Dillon shifted his gaze back to Kiera and touched the brim of his cowboy hat. "You must be Kiera."

"I—" She swallowed, then held her hand out. "Yes. Nice to meet you."

"Likewise. Clair's told me a lot of nice things about you." Dillon took Kiera's hand, held it, then narrowed his eyes. "Have we met before?"

"No." Shaking her head, she pulled her hand away. "I think I just have one of those faces."

"Hardly." Grinning, Dillon looked at Sam. "Better keep an eye on her. I'm a happily married man, but there's more than one randy rancher out there who'll try and steal her away."

"They can try," Sam said evenly, but with enough heat behind his words to make Kiera blush. Just the thought of another man sniffing around her made him want to skip the party altogether and drag her back to the hotel where they could be alone.

"I appreciate you having me here today." Kiera's obvious change of conversation wasn't lost on Sam. "Clair told me your ranch was amazing, but that doesn't begin to describe it."

"Thanks." Dillon shrugged off the compliment. "I'd take you on a tour, but if I don't deliver you both to Clair pronto, I'll be in the doghouse with her. Sam's been to the ranch a couple of times. I'm sure he wouldn't mind showing you around."

Sam nodded, remembered a private little spot behind the barn where he and Kiera could be alone for a few minutes. "I can manage that."

"Great." Dillon gestured to the entryway. "After you, m'lady."

It wasn't just the house and grounds that were amazing, Kiera thought when they stepped outside. Clair had told her that half the town would be here, but it looked more like the *entire* town. Clusters of people packed the large stone patio and spilled over onto an expanse of lawn the size of a baseball field, where the band, a dance floor and long wooden tables had been set up. The conversation and laughter pulsing from the crowd was almost as loud as the live music.

"Looks like Clair got waylaid by Madge," Dillon said when he spotted her on the other side of the crowded dance floor. "Let me get you drinks, then I'll go save her."

"I've got it." Sam waved Dillon on. "Clair needs you more than we do."

"Isn't that the woman from the diner?" Kiera asked after Dillon had left, leaning in close so she could be heard over the band's fast-paced rendition of "Norma Jean Riley." "The one with six sons?"

"That's Madge." Grinning, Sam nodded at the food tables. "And that's her husband, Pete, standing by the ribs with their three youngest boys."

They were all tall and lanky, Kiera noted, recognizing the teenager who'd waited on her. He was a cute kid, but at the risk of staining her dress, she decided she'd wait to say hello when he didn't have a drink or food in his hands.

Sam lowered his head. "What's your pleasure?"

She shivered at his question and the warmth of his breath on her neck. The rise of heat in her blood had nothing to do with the late afternoon temperature. She angled her head so her lips were close to his ear and whispered, "Whatever you're having."

She watched his jaw tighten and his eyes darken, felt the air crackle between them. She'd never been so bold before, but there'd never been anyone like Sam before, either.

"Don't move," he demanded. "And don't talk to any strange men when I'm gone."

"What if someone says hello to me?" she teased, enjoyed the sudden tic in the corner of Sam's eye. "I wouldn't want to be rude."

"Manners are highly overrated. But just in case anyone's watching—"

He shocked her by slipping an arm around her shoulders and kissing her on the mouth. Not hard enough or long enough to be scandalous, but enough to brand her as his. And then, just as abruptly, he dropped his arm away and hurried off.

Still in a daze, her lips still tingling, Kiera wandered to the edge of the crowd and watched the flow of people. The spread of food that had been laid out to the left of the patio could feed a small country, she noted. Six barbecues made from large, round oil drums grilled a continuous procession of steaks, ribs and chicken, and vats of sweet corn on the cob and baked beans were refilled every few minutes. There were at least four different salads, three different breads and a table of pies, cakes and cookies that would tempt the taste buds of the most determined dieter.

She was still trying to absorb the fact that she was actually here, at the Blackhawk Ranch, when a little boy suddenly bumped into her, yanking her from her thoughts.

"Sorry!" the child yelled, then chased after three other boys.

Kiera watched the youngster run off, remembered playing with her sisters and brother when she was that age. She missed them, she realized. If she'd learned nothing else coming here to Wolf River, it was how desperately important her family was to her. How much she needed them.

Her gaze shifted to Sam, who was currently making his way toward her with two bottles of beer. He winked at her when their eyes met, and her heart skipped. As she watched him approach, she realized it wasn't only her family she needed.

Now that she'd met Sam and fallen in love with him, she needed so much more.

"Nathaniel Joseph, you apologize to this woman right now."

Kiera looked over at the blonde who'd come up behind her. The woman's blouse was fireball-red, her jeans Versace, and she had a complexion that belonged in a skin-care advertisement. Beside her, Kiera recognized the little dark-haired boy who'd bumped into her a moment ago.

"Aw, Mom, I said I was sorry," he mumbled, his eyes downcast.

"It's really not necessary—"

"Oh, yes, it is." The woman pursed her lips and looked at her son. "Nathan?"

"I'm sorry I bumped into you," the child said, lifting his gaze.

"And?" the blonde prompted.

The little boy scratched his head and thought, then grinned. "And it won't happen again?"

The woman nodded in approval. "Now introduce yourself."

Proud of himself now, the child stuck out his hand. "How do you do," he said with practiced politeness. "My name is Nathan Blackhawk."

Blackhawk? Breath held, Kiera took the child's small hand. "How do you do, Nathan. My name is Kiera Daniels."

"You're Kiera Daniels?" Smiling, the woman held out her hand, too. "I'm Julianna Blackhawk. My husband, Lucas, is Clair's cousin. We've heard so much about you."

Kiera glanced nervously toward Sam, saw that he'd been stopped by an older couple wearing patriotic T-shirts and cowboy boots to match. "About me?"

"Can I go now?" Nathan whined.

"No more running into people," Julianna admonished, then shook her head with a sigh when he dashed off. "The Blackhawk children certainly aren't making a good first impression."

"It really was an accident." Kiera watched the boy join up with the other children and jump around like a little monkey. "He's adorable."

"You wouldn't have said that yesterday when he and his two sisters thought it would be neat to turn our cat into a sparkle kitty." But there was a hint of laughter in Julianna's eyes. "I suspect I'll be combing glue out of the cat's fur and vacuuming up glitter for the next year."

In spite of the nerves rattling up and down her spine, Kiera couldn't help but laugh. Children had always been a complete mystery to her. She'd been so busy with school and working that she'd never even thought about having a family of her own. But as she glanced at Sam, watched him break free from the people he'd been talking to, she thought about it now. Wondered what kind of father he'd make. What their children might look like…

"Clair is quite impressed with you," Julianna said. "She says employees like you are rare. 'One in a million,' I think were her exact words."

If only Julianna knew how accurate that statement was, Kiera thought. The guilt seeped in again, as did the overwhelming need to tell these people who she really was. But she couldn't. Not here, not today.

Not ever.

"I've never worked for anyone like Clair before." Kiera was glad she could finally be truthful about something. "It's unusual for the owner of a large hotel or restaurant to know the names of the staff, let alone invite them to parties."

"We all agree she's pretty special." A smile lit Julianna's eyes. "Rand and Seth are certainly happy she's settling here in Wolf River. It's so wonderful to see them all together again. And now with Dillon moving back here, too, it feels complete."

"Why did they all leave?" Kiera hoped her question sounded casual when, in fact, her hands were trembling.

"Long story." Julianna flicked a glance toward her son, watched him tumble on the lawn with the other children. "And complicated. Damn, grass stains are a bitch."

Complicated. Exactly the word Sam had used that day in Clair's office. Obviously, something had happened in this family's past they didn't discuss.

Kiera knew exactly what that was like.

"I understand she's working on you to stay here, as well." Julianna turned her attention back to Kiera. "Any chance you might?"

"I'm afraid not." Kiera shook her head. "But I enjoyed working at the Four Winds."

"There are definite advantages." Julianna smiled at Sam when he successfully made it past a throng of boot-scooting dancers. "Hello, Sam. I was just talking about you."

"Is that so?" He leaned over to kiss Julianna's cheek, then handed a longneck to Kiera. "Should I ask?"

"Much more fun to keep you guessing." Julianna slid one arm through Sam's and the other through Kiera's. "Come on, let's go join the others. I want Kiera to meet the whole motley crew."

Heart racing, her nerves stretched razor thin, Kiera let Julianna escort her across the patio toward a table where the Blackhawk family had gathered. One by one, she shook their hands. Rand, with his reserved gaze and black eyes. Seth, with his quick smile and slash of dark brow. And then Lucas, Julianna's husband, a cousin, Kiera remembered. The resemblance between them all was remarkable, she thought. A testament to the strength and power of the Blackhawk blood.

With Sam by her side, she met the wives and some of the children, and when Clair and Dillon joined the group, it felt as if a circle had been completed.

A circle she didn't belong in, she knew, easing back while they all teased each other and laughed among themselves. They'd welcomed her warmly and openly, been nothing but kind and generous. It no longer mattered to her who William Blackhawk had been, or what he'd done. Kiera knew in her heart that these were good people. People she could not intrude upon, or bring her troubles to.

When Sam brushed the small of her back with his hand, she glanced up at him, saw him watching her with a curious expression. Her entire life she'd always been good at getting what she wanted, had learned to be strong and work hard to accomplish any goal she set her mind and heart on.

For the first time, she realized she couldn't have everything she wanted. Couldn't have the one thing she wanted more than her next breath.

She would leave, but not without telling Sam the truth. Not the whole truth but hopefully enough so that he would at least understand why she'd deceived him.

"Sounds like a two-step," he said when the band struck up John Michael Montgomery's, "Be My Baby Tonight." "Think you can keep up with me?"

Smiling, she put her hand on his shoulder. "Mister, I'll leave you panting in the dust."

"Darlin'—" he dragged her against him "—you'll be begging for mercy after one round."

"A little less talk," she said, quoting the song, then laughed when he swung her around, certain that her heart had wings.

Somehow, she kept up with him, and he with her, on the dance floor and later, much later, in bed, until they were both panting, both begging for mercy.

And in the wee hours of the morning, lying in his arms, Kiera couldn't help but think how they'd both lost.

Ten

"You've got a fine hotel here, Sammy, a damn fine hotel. Growing faster than a cat with its tail on fire."

Sam didn't mind the slap on the back from Tyke Madden, especially considering he was the president of the Cattlemen's Association that currently filled the Four Winds Hotel. Still, Sam couldn't help but wince inwardly at the man's use of the name, "Sammy."

"The Four Winds is at your complete disposal, Tyke."

"Hell, I ain't gonna be disposing of nothing." Tyke chewed on an unlit cigar, then hitched up his suit pants. "You keep feedin' us boys grub like you did this morning, and I'll be wearing my expand-os to meals."

Tyke Madden was one of the "good-ol-boys" from way back. The barrel-chested, cigar-chewing cattleman was wealthy, outspoken and influential. If Tyke came away from the conference happy, then everyone would be happy. Which meant more business for the Four Winds.

Smiling, Sam turned to Mrs. Tyke Madden, a platinum blonde who'd been a stripper thirty years ago and damn proud of it. "Have you booked your massage and facial yet, Amanda?"

"Sweetcheeks, I got me a two-hour appointment with Michael in twenty minutes." Too many years of cigarettes gave her voice a throaty growl. "I expect to be naked and on the table in ten."

The woman was in her fifties, but talk was she'd kept her great figure by installing a pole in the Madden master bedroom.

"I'll call the spa and make sure he's ready for you," Sam offered.

"Hell," Tyke guffawed and gave his wife a hug. "Ain't nobody ever ready for my little sugarbug. Better make sure that Michael has health insurance."

Sam thought it best not to comment on that.

"Honeybear." Amanda squinted her eyes. "Don't we know that girl over there?"

Sam looked in the direction Amanda's gaze had taken and spotted Kiera coming in through the hotel's double glass doors. When he'd left her motel room at three this morning, he'd made her promise to have lunch with him at two o'clock today. *Right on time,* he thought, glancing at his watch. Most women would have made him wait, but he'd learned from the beginning that Kiera was not most women.

"Sugarbug, you know I never look at other women," Tyke said, though everyone knew he had a roving eye.

"I never forget a face or a name, which was quite handy in my previous line of work," Amanda said with a wink, then slipped on the glasses she kept attached to a sequined lanyard around her neck. "I swear I've seen that girl somewhere before, though it's been a long while."

Was it possible? Sam watched Kiera smile at the doorman as she walked past, then glanced back at Amanda, who was tapping her chin.

"*A…b…c…*" She paused, narrowing her eyes in thought. "No, not *c,* it's *K.* Karen…Kate…Kirsten…"

Sam stiffened. "Kiera?"

"That's it." Amanda snapped her fingers. "Now let's see, her last name—"

"Daniels," Sam supplied.

Amanda stared at Kiera, who was heading toward Adagio's. "I don't think so," she said, then glanced at her watch. "Oh, hell, gotta go. Don't wanna be late for Mike. Come on, honeybear, walk me to the spa."

Dammit! Sam watched the couple walk away and it was all he could do not to grab the woman by the arms and stop her, beg her to remember.

Later, he decided, and started toward the restaurant. It would be easy enough to invite Amanda and Tyke for drinks in the bar. Maybe a nice glass of Glenlivet would help the woman's memory.

He imagined that Kiera wouldn't appreciate his inquiries, but after spending yesterday afternoon with Kiera at the barbecue, then making love with her again last night, he knew he couldn't just let her walk out of his life. Not now.

Not ever.

The thought staggered him. He'd never felt that way about any woman before. Had never considered…

God, he couldn't even say it in his mind.

"Sammy—"

Sam turned at the sound of Amanda's call and her heels clicking as she ran across the marbled floor toward him. "Sweetcheeks," she said brightly, "I just remembered her last name."

Kiera sipped a glass of ice water, thinking how strange it felt to be sitting in Adagio's among the other patrons rather than waiting on their tables. The hostess, a college student named Ginger, had given her a big hug when she'd walked in, but the restaurant was so busy there'd been no time for anything more than a quick hello before she'd been escorted to a booth in the back of the restaurant. Kiera knew she wouldn't have had a table at all if Sam hadn't reserved it for them.

It seemed odd how familiar Adagio's felt to her considering the short time she'd worked here. The scent of the rosemary and olive bread, the feel of the crisp linen napkins, the classical music that softly drifted across the room, repeating itself every hour. More than familiar, she thought, watching the waiters balance trays of food and the diners enjoying themselves. It was comfortable. As if she'd been here all her life.

She glanced across the restaurant, watching for Sam to walk in. He was easy to spot, not only because he was taller than most men, and disturbingly handsome, but because she'd developed an internal radar system when he was close. The closer he got, the more her system jangled its alarm.

No sign of him.

She sipped her water again, then dropped her hands into her lap to twist her napkin. He was obviously running a little late. On the first day of a conference, it made sense he'd be tied up taking care of a hundred little problems. But he'd be here. She was certain of that. As each second passed, her stomach knotted just a little bit tighter.

Truth time.

She'd spent the morning carefully wording her speech, had paced the living room while she recited it out loud. She would tell him why she'd come here. Why she couldn't stay. But she couldn't, wouldn't, tell him who she was.

He'd press her on the point, of course. Which was why she'd decided to tell him here, while they were at lunch. She knew he couldn't yell or try to intimidate her or even show his irritation. There were too many hotel guests watching, not to mention employees. He'd pretend that everything was fine, figuring that when they were alone later, she'd break under his badgering, or maybe even his kisses, and tell him her name.

What he wouldn't know is that she wouldn't be here later. She'd already checked out of the motel. Her bags were in her car she'd valeted. When lunch was over, she was going to drive away from Wolf River. From the Blackhawk family and from the man she loved.

"Kiera?"

She jumped at the sound of Ginger's whispered voice, saw the hostess standing by the table. Her brow was furrowed tightly; her gaze darted back nervously toward the kitchen.

"What's wrong?" Kiera reached out and touched the hostess on the arm, could feel her trembling.

"Chef Phillipe," she said, keeping her voice low. "He's on a rampage, much worse than usual."

"Ginger, I don't work here anymore."

"I know." The hostess bit her lip. "But you're the only one here who's ever stood up to him and I thought that maybe, at least until Sam could get here, that you could do something?"

"Where's Christine?" Kiera glanced around the busy restaurant, looking for the manager.

"That's the problem," Ginger said, her voice shaking. "He's got her cornered in the kitchen, yelling at her. Something about getting fired."

Oh, God, Kiera groaned inwardly. Obviously the man had found out about that he was about to get canned and he was taking it out on the manager.

A pregnant woman.

Kiera threw her napkin on the table, then slid out of the booth and hurried through the restaurant, but not enough to draw attention. *Why today?*

But when she stepped into the kitchen, every thought of Sam and their lunch date flew out of her mind.

Christina, her face pale and her eyes wide, was pressed between a work counter and a sink while Chef Phillipe berated her. Tyler and two other servers and Robert were staring wide-eyed and dazed, too stunned to move.

The bastard!

"This restaurant will be nothing without me, I will

sue you all, every last one of you, you are all *bon pour rien,* incompetent—"

"Get away from her right now, *imbécile!*"

The chef whirled around, then froze when he saw who had dared call him a stupid baboon—and in French, nonetheless!

"You!" Eyes bulging, he moved away from Christina. "*Que faites-vous ici?* And who are *you* to tell *me* what to do?"

"You're a coward and a bully." Kiera egged him on so he would move farther away from the manager. "You shame your profession and you shame yourself."

"You do not speak to Chef Phillipe this way!" His face bright red, Phillipe moved menacingly toward Kiera. "You *idiot sans valeur,* worthless idiot. You will leave my kitchen immediately."

"Funny," Kiera said as if she were bored. "I heard it wasn't your kitchen anymore."

When Phillipe's eyes bulged, Christina stepped forward. "Kiera, don't—"

"Get out of here, Christina," Kiera said calmly without taking her eyes off the chef. "Now."

Christina glanced from Phillipe to Kiera. "But—"

"Now," Kiera repeated firmly and the manager quickly backed out of the kitchen.

"You *dare* to come in here and speak to me with such impertinence," Phillipe hissed, moving closer to Kiera, his hands clenched into tight fists. "Who do you think you are?"

Kiera reached for a cast-iron frying pan sitting on the counter beside her, then held it up. "I'm the one who's going to bean that fat head of yours if you take one more step toward me."

Phillipe hesitated, then made a choking sound and charged at her like a mad bull. Adrenaline running, poised for battle, she raised the pan, knew she could easily duck out of the stocky man's way and give him a rap on the back of his head that would send him spinning.

She wasn't certain what happened next; it happened too quickly. But suddenly she was staring at Sam's broad back, and the chef was laid out on the floor.

Sam had punched Phillipe!

"Thanks," she mumbled, "but I really didn't—"

Sam spun and grabbed her shoulders. Anger flared in his eyes and nostrils. "What the hell were you thinking?"

"He had Christine backed into a corner." Her blood was still pumping fast, and she had a death grip on the frying pan in her hand. "She's seven months pregnant, for God's sake. What was I supposed to do?"

His hands tightened painfully on her arms, then with an oath he released her and turned back to Phillipe, who lay wailing on the floor that his nose was broken and he was going to sue.

"Shut up or I'll break something else," Sam threatened.

Rage, blood-red, white-hot, raced through Sam's veins. He stared at Phillipe, wished to God that the man would say something, *anything,* to give him an excuse to hit him again. But other than some quiet whimpering in French, the chef had stilled.

Sam glared at the waiters and sous-chef, who stood huddled by a stove. "What the hell happened here?"

It was Robert who took a cautious step forward. "He

was ranting about calling a lawyer and how he had a contract so nobody could fire him, and when Christine came into the kitchen, he started yelling at her."

Sam grabbed Phillipe by the scruff of his neck and hauled him up, struggled with the urge to punch him again, just for good measure. "How did you find out you were going to be let go?"

"I saw the letter on Clair's desk this afternoon." His voice was a nasally whine.

"Clair wasn't in her office this afternoon." Sam tightened his grip on the man. "And she sure as hell wouldn't leave a letter of termination lying on her desk."

Phillipe's pain-filled eyes widened when Sam brought his thumb and forefinger toward the chef's nose. "I was looking in a drawer for a pencil, that's all," the chef said in a rush. "I just happened to see a file with my name on it."

"You're as bad a liar as you are a chef." As much as he wanted to inflict further pain on the man, Sam simply shoved him away. Phillipe stumbled backward but managed to stay on his feet.

"Not that it matters." Sam shook his head in disgust. "You won't be able to get a job at a hot dog stand when this gets out."

"I am Chef Phillipe!" The wounded man straightened indignantly. Blood dripped from his nose onto his white apron. "I have prepared meals for royalty, been awarded culinary honors. Working in this kitchen, with your inept staff, has been beneath me. I will own this miserable hotel by the time my lawyers are through. I will—"

When Sam took a step toward the chef, he shrank back and his hands instantly shot up to protect his nose. "Tell it to the judge," Sam said. "Maybe if you're nice, he'll let you prepare meals for the other inmates in your cell. Now let's go and have a nice chat with the sheriff. He's waiting for us out back."

Sam looked at Kiera and shook off the image of Phillipe coming at her. "We'll talk after I deal with this," he said tightly, saw her eyes narrow with irritation. "Not *one* word, Kiera. Not now. Just be here when I get back."

She wanted to argue, he could see the fire in her eyes and that signature lift of her pretty little chin. He breathed a sigh of relief when she nodded. At least there was *one* less problem to deal with, he thought, then glanced around the kitchen at all the stunned staff who'd filed in to watch the action.

"Get the orders out that you can and stall until I get back," he barked. "We'll have to shut down hot foods for now and see if we can squeak by with salads and sandwiches."

He heard the grumbles and moans and ignored them all as he escorted a protesting Phillipe through the back door of the kitchen to the waiting squad car.

"I'll come down and make a statement as soon as I can break away." Sam handed the irate chef to Rafe Duncan, Wolf River's sheriff. "But you can start with two charges of assault, the first one being Christine Desmond."

The sheriff's face turned hard as a rock. "Is she all right?"

"Just scared. She's with Clair."

The sheriff pulled his handcuffs off his belt. "I have a sister named Christine Desmond. Brunette, pregnant, manages the restaurant. Wouldn't happen to be the same one, would it?"

Already knowing the answer, Chef Phillipe groaned. "I have my rights—"

"We'll get around to your rights soon enough." The sheriff clamped the handcuffs on Phillipe and gave them a tug that made the chef yelp. "You said there were two assaults."

"I'll get back to you on the second one," Sam said. "I've got to handle damage control right now."

"I'll be waitin' for you." The sheriff shoved the distraught chef into the back seat of the squad car. Phillipe was sweating profusely.

Heading back to the kitchen, Sam swore viciously with every step. *Of all the damn times for this to happen.* The hotel would be all right in catering, they had a full staff there because of the conference. But an entire week without a chef in their fine dining restaurant would greatly upset the guests looking for a meal away from the banquet food. *Dammit!*

And if that weren't enough, not even ten minutes ago he'd found out about Kiera. Who she really was and why she'd come to Wolf River.

His mind was still reeling from it. But as much as he wanted to drag her out of that kitchen and up to his office to hash it out, he couldn't deal with that now.

He stood outside the kitchen entrance, resisted the urge to kick the door open. The kitchen staff would look to him now for direction. He had to set the tone, keep everyone calm. He combed his fingers through his hair, then straightened his jacket.

Kiera better damn well be where he'd left her, he thought irritably. If he had to chase her down, there'd be hell to pay.

Calmly, quietly, he pushed open the door, narrowed his eyes when he saw she wasn't standing by the salad station where he'd left her. He gritted his teeth, prepared himself to go after her. But then he saw her. Wearing an apron, her hair clipped on top of her head, she stood at the grill.

Cooking.

"Salmon up in two," she yelled out, sprinkling herbs on the fish with her right hand while she dumped pasta into boiling water with her left.

"I need plates," she yelled over her shoulder at one of the busboys. "*Platos, por favor.* Tyler, what's your ticket?"

"Picatta, no capers." Tyler called out the order while he assembled a salad. "Table fifteen wants a side of marinara."

"Robert, you take it," Kiera shouted to the sous-chef. "Watch your basil and add a kiss of red wine. I need those plates now!"

Arms loaded with plates, a busboy hurried from the dishwasher to the grill station while two of the servers scurried about.

"Hot plate." One server zigged while the other zagged.

"Order up, six." Kiera slipped the salmon onto a plate and drizzled it with a sauce she'd had simmering in a pan. "Filet's in oven."

Dumbfounded, Sam stared. He'd obviously been in kitchens before, many times, but as he watched Kiera work with the staff, he felt a rhythm like never before. Like a choreographed dance, he thought.

"Split order ready in one," she called out and scooped up an order of penne onto two plates. "Rico, cut me more tomatoes, pronto, pronto. Robert, if you add a little cream to that sauce, that pretty girl at table six will want to have sex with you. *I'll* want to have sex with you," she added, which made Robert laugh and turn bright red.

Sam raised an eyebrow but stayed back, watching the show. The orders flew at her, but she never faltered, never hesitated, somehow managed to do six things at once and keep track of the rest of the kitchen, too.

Apparently she'd done this before.

There'd been clues all along, he thought. Her expertise in the front of the restaurant, her observations of Phillipe. He'd watched her cook before, once at her motel, then the soufflé in his suite. She'd told him she *liked* to cook, and when he'd been eavesdropping the day she'd been hired, he remembered she'd told Janet that she'd had *some* kitchen training.

Obviously, she'd had a great deal more than *some* training.

How obtuse could he be? Just when he thought he knew who she was, he realized he didn't have a clue.

Amazement, admiration and annoyance all meshed inside of him, then settled in his gut like a lump of concrete.

He stepped back out of the kitchen before she saw him. Obviously she had the kitchen under control, and for now he'd let her work.

Turning, he headed for Clair's office.

* * *

"Kiera, that was amazing." Two glasses of red wine in his hands, Robert followed Kiera out of the kitchen. "*You* are amazing."

"Thanks, partner." She sank down in the same corner booth where she'd sat almost eight hours ago, waiting for Sam. It felt like a lifetime had passed since then. "You're pretty amazing yourself."

She took the wine Robert offered her and they clinked glasses.

The dimly lit restaurant was quiet now, with only a few diners still straggling over desserts and drinks. As of ten minutes ago, the kitchen was officially closed for the night.

It was the first time today she'd had a chance to sit down. Her feet were throbbing, her shoulders were aching and marsala sauce stained the front of her tan slacks.

She couldn't remember when she'd been happier.

"You were so right about cutting back on the thyme and adding the cumin in the house chicken." Robert leaned forward, his face bright. "And you still have to show me how you made your rémoulade, that was awesome. And your marsala, I would kill for that recipe."

While Robert went on, Kiera simply smiled and sipped her wine. Robert had been bullied by Phillipe for so long, he'd lost his love of cooking. It warmed her heart to see the passion in his eyes and hear the exhilaration in his voice.

"You're going to make a wonderful chef, Robert." She raised her glass to him. "Don't ever let anyone tell you that you won't."

Robert lowered his gaze and stared at his glass of wine. "I—I'm sorry about earlier today. When Phillipe was yelling at Christine and then he came at you, I just froze."

"Don't even think about it." She reached across the table and laid her hand on Robert's. "Believe me when I tell you I've dealt with bigger, tougher men than Phillipe Girard."

"Actually," Robert said awkwardly, "I, well, none of the staff here know exactly *what* to believe about you. There was all kinds of talk before, but after today, well…you can imagine."

"I certainly can." But the fact was, she didn't care. She had a much bigger, much more immediate problem to deal with than what the staff at Adagio's thought of her.

Sam was waiting to speak to her.

Tyler had given her the message ten minutes ago. It was short and to the point: *Meet me in my office.*

He hadn't even said pretty please.

She'd seen him when he'd come back to the kitchen after hauling Phillipe outside, had been surprised that he hadn't said one word to her. She'd worried that he might even close the restaurant until another chef could be brought in. But he hadn't. He watched her, then backed away and let her work.

He'd trusted her. And the fact that he had made her load of guilt twice as heavy.

"I've got to go now, Robert." She drew her hand away and stood. "Just don't forget what I said. You're going to make one hell of a chef."

She left him sitting there, left Adagio's, and couldn't

bear to look back. She knew this would be the last time she'd be here.

To avoid the crowds of rambunctious cattlemen milling around the hotel, she took the service elevator to the sixth floor and stepped out when the doors *swished* open. The hallway was empty and deathly quiet.

Sucking in a deep breath of courage, she opened the outer door to Sam's office and stepped inside. It was dark, but the inner office door was ajar and a soft sliver of light shimmered through the crack. She moved toward it. *You can do this.*

When she pushed the door open, then stepped inside the dimly lit office, she saw him standing at the window, arms folded as he stared out into the darkness.

"Sam."

He turned, moved out of the shadows toward her.

"Please, just stay over there. I'll never get through this if you don't." She had to say what she needed to say all at once, or she was certain she'd fall apart. She kept her gaze locked with Sam's, refused to let herself look away. "You know I haven't been completely honest with you, that I've kept things from you."

"Kiera—"

"Sam, *please.*" She held up a hand to stop him. "Let me talk."

He clamped his jaw shut.

"I wasn't running from an abusive relationship, which I let you believe," she began, "but I told you the truth about the black eye. I did fall off a horse, which is actually quite embarrassing, considering I was raised on a horse ranch in East Texas."

Hoping that she could hold herself together, she folded her arms. "I have two older sisters, twins, and a brother who's bossy and over-protective and—"

When Sam started to speak again, she shook her head. "And in spite of the fact that I found out they, and my own mother, have been deceiving me my entire life, I love them all very much."

It felt good to say it, she realized. She'd been so angry, mostly with Trey, and she didn't want to be angry anymore. She was too tired, too weary from all the lies.

"I went to culinary school in New York straight from high school," she said. "After I graduated I travelled and worked around the country before I went back to New York. For the past two years I've been a chef at a popular new restaurant—" she almost said the name, but caught herself in time. Even now, there were things she couldn't, didn't dare, tell him. "Four months ago, on a whim, I applied for an assistant's position with a world-renowned chef in Paris. I was shocked when they actually hired me, but it was the opportunity of a lifetime, so of course I accepted. I quit my job, spent two weeks on my family's ranch and scheduled in three weeks' vacation time to spend in Paris before I started my new job."

She pressed her fingers to her temple, rubbed at the threatening headache, then went on, "The night before I was ready to leave, I overheard my brother and one of my sisters arguing in the kitchen. They thought I'd already gone to bed, but I was too wound up to sleep and I'd come back downstairs. When I heard my name mentioned, I listened."

It seemed like a hundred years ago, but she could still hear the whispered quarrel, Alaina's frustration and Trey's unbending resolve.

You have to tell her the truth, Trey. You've already waited too long. If she finds out on her own—

She won't find out. We'll let her get settled in Paris, have a good time. I'll tell her in a few months.

You've been saying that for the past four years. Dammit, she's not a child anymore. She has a right to know the truth. Will you stop being so bullheaded and just tell her?

Kiera pushed the memory from her mind, forced herself to concentrate on the present, on this moment. *You're almost there,* she told herself.

"When I finally stepped into the kitchen and confronted them, my brother refused to talk to me, so my sister told me." Kiera could still see worry in Alaina's eyes, hear the pain in her voice. "She told me that my father had never married my mother. That he had abandoned us all when I was three. All those years I thought he was dead, he was living here, in Wolf River. Married, with a family."

"Kiera, please." Sam's mouth pressed into a hard line. "You don't need to tell me this."

"But I do." She opened her eyes, prayed he could see into her heart. "Don't you see? I was lying, too. Just like my mother had lied, just like my sisters and brother. I don't want to lie anymore. Not to you, Sam. You've been the most wonderful thing that's ever happened to me."

She stepped toward him. "Being with you—"

"Kiera, stop—"

"Making love with you," she whispered.

"God, Kiera, *stop!*"

She did stop, the urgency in his voice, the fierce expression on his face, confusing her. From the corner of her eye, she spotted movement in the far, darkened corner of the room. Breath held, she turned.

Oh dear God.

She watched in horror as her brother stepped out of the shadows.

Eleven

Violence glinted in Trey Blackhawk's dark eyes; Sam recognized the look only too well. But the violence wasn't directed at Kiera, Sam knew. It was directed at him.

No question about it, he thought, accepting, and bracing himself for, the inevitable. After what Kiera's brother had just heard, there was going to be hell to pay.

"Trey." Kiera's voice was barely audible in the wire-tight silence. "What are you, how did you—"

"I called him this afternoon." Sam stepped closer to Trey and Kiera. "Just before Phillipe's tirade in the kitchen."

Brow furrowed, Kiera shook her head as she glanced from Trey back to Sam. "I—I don't understand."

"One of the guests at the Four Winds spotted you coming into the hotel today and recognized you."

Amanda had been extremely accommodating once she'd remembered Kiera's name. "She met you a few years ago when they bought a couple of yearlings from your family's ranch."

"Amanda and Tyke Madden." Shades of light and dark cut across the sharp angles of Trey's face as he spoke. "You were home from school at the time. I'm sure you remember them. 'Honeybear and Sugarbug'?"

"Oh. Right." Slowly, Kiera's gaze swiveled back to Sam; her eyes narrowed to slits. "Wait. Did you say you *called* my brother?"

"I thought he should know where you were."

"You *thought?*" Hands thrust on her hips, Kiera rounded on him. "What gives you the right to interfere in my family business? Just because we slept together—"

The low growl rumbled from Trey's throat just before his arm swung out and clipped Sam's jaw. If Sam hadn't been expecting the blow, he might have gone down.

Kiera squeaked, then jumped between the two men, but Sam brushed her away in case the "discussion" escalated. Dammit! He didn't want to fight over a man's right to defend his sister's honor.

"I'll give you that one, Blackhawk." Damn, but the man packed a punch. "The next one I'll have to take payment."

"Go for it." Trey stepped close again, locked eyes with Sam. "What the hell kind of man takes advantage of a vulnerable woman?"

"Trey Blackhawk!" Kiera squirmed in between the two men, who stood nose to nose. "That's none of your business! I'm a grown woman, for God's sake. Stop this right now."

A muscle jumped in Trey's jaw, but slowly, reluctantly, he eased back, then turned to Kiera.

"What were you thinking?" Trey admonished. "What could you possibly hope to gain from coming to Wolf River?"

"You wouldn't talk to me, even Alaina shut me out, told me to wait. Wait for what?" She threw out her hands. "The truth fairy to appear in my bedroom one night and slip a note under my pillow? Yes, I wanted to know who William Blackhawk was, I wanted to see where he lived. I wanted to understand why he destroyed our mother and how he could leave all of us, his own children, without so much as an it's-been-great-but-go-to-hell."

Eyes glistening, Kiera reached out and took hold of her brother's arms. The desperation in her voice, the raw pain, almost had Sam reaching for her. But he couldn't. However this unfolded between sister and brother, he knew he couldn't step between them.

"*Why,* Trey?" Kiera's knuckles turned white on Trey's arms. "Why won't you tell me the truth about our father? The whole truth. What are you still holding back from me?"

"William Blackhawk was a bastard." Trey's lip curled. "That's all you need to know."

"That *isn't* all I need to know," she said on a low sob. "I have a right to know, dammit, *tell me.*"

"I'll tell you."

Sam whipped his head around and saw Clair standing in the doorway.

* * *

This isn't happening, Kiera thought wildly. *None of this is real.*

Her heart jumped into her throat when Clair stepped into the room. The look in her eyes, distant and cold, shimmered in the dim light of Sam's office.

Kiera's hands slipped from Trey's arms and she turned on knees that threatened to buckle.

"Clair, I'm sorry." Kiera swallowed the lump in her throat. "I'm so sorry. I never wanted you to know about me, about my father."

"Sam—" Clair moved closer to Kiera "—would you turn up the light please?"

A chill shivered up Kiera's spine as Clair's eyes met hers. When the light filled the room, Clair studied Kiera's face, looked at her as if she'd never seen her before.

"There'd always been something I couldn't put my finger on," Clair said quietly. "A connection I didn't understand. It's subtle, but I can see it now. The shape of your eyes." Clair's gaze shifted to Trey. "You could almost be Rand's twin, you look so much alike. Your name is Trey, I believe I heard Kiera say?"

Trey nodded. Neither offered a hand.

"You knew my father?" Kiera asked, ignoring the hand that Trey put on her arm.

Clair shook her head. "I was born in Wolf River, but I wasn't raised here. I grew up in South Carolina, lived there until I met Jacob and moved back here a few months ago."

"South Carolina?" Confused, Kiera glanced at Sam, but he'd retreated from this family drama playing out, and she couldn't blame him. Kiera had brought this on herself, but now that she had, she'd see it through.

"After my parents died in a car accident, I was adopted. So were Rand and Seth. Rand was raised on a small ranch in West Texas and Seth in New Mexico."

"But you had other family here," Kiera said. "Why were you separated and adopted?"

"I'll tell her."

It was Trey who spoke. His iron-hard expression frightened Kiera, and suddenly she wasn't feeling like a grown woman at all. She felt like a child. Helpless and scared and alone.

"There were three Blackhawk brothers, full-blood Cherokee." Trey's tone was void of all emotion. "Thomas, who was Lucas's father. Jonathan, who was Rand, Seth and Clair's father. Then there was William, Dillon's father."

"And our father," Kiera added, digging her fingernails into her fisted palms.

"William alienated himself from his brothers after they married white women." Disgust edged Trey's words. "He considered their children impure."

"But that makes no sense." Kiera could barely hear over the buzzing in her head. "Our mother is white."

"She was the forbidden fruit," Trey said. "Which made her all the more tempting. She was a pretty young widow when he met her, living on a ranch in a tiny border town almost four hundred miles from Wolf River. Who would ever know? He told her up front how it would be, paid off her bills and visited often, let her tell the town they had gotten married, even let her have his children. But he never intended to marry her."

Kiera wanted to hate her mother for being so weak, for letting a man use her like that. But she could only pity her.

"After a few years," Trey went on, "she became a burden to him, *we* became a burden. He gave her a choice, accept one big check and never say anything, or he'd leave her with nothing. She had four children, what could she do? She took the money, then concocted a story of how he drowned saving a little boy's life, told the story so many times that, in her mind, it became a reality. Now, in her confused mind, she actually believes that story."

Growing up, Kiera had learned not to ask too many questions about her father. She'd understood that the wrong word or comment could send her mother into her darkened bedroom for weeks on end, heavily sedated. Kiera had heard the doctor whisper "mental break-down," but it was years before she really understood what it meant.

From the time he was a teenager, Trey had always been the patriarch of their family. He'd taken care of everyone and run the ranch, too, but with an iron fist. Kiera had swung from hating him one minute, to adoring him the next. She looked at him now, under-stood why he'd been so angry his entire life, why he'd tried to protect them all. He'd known their father hadn't died, but he'd let everyone, including their mother, believe the lie.

The truth hung in the air, ice-cold; Kiera felt it shiver in her bones. And she knew there was more. "Our father's the reason Clair and her brothers were separated and adopted out, isn't he?"

"He told everyone we'd died in the accident." Clair wrapped her arms around her waist, as if she might protect the child growing inside her from the ugliness of her words. "William Blackhawk was wealthy and influential. He knew how to manipulate people, pay them off to make things happen. Rand and Seth were just little boys, they thought their family was dead. I was a toddler, too little to remember anything more than images and feelings. We all found each other a few months ago and we're making up for lost time."

Lost time? Kiera thought. How could you make up for that much lost time? Bile rose in her throat and she closed her eyes, could only imagine what Clair and her brothers had endured at William Blackhawk's hands.

Kiera turned and looked up at her brother. "How do you know about Clair and her brothers, what our father did to them? How *could* you know?"

"I hired a private investigator two months ago," he said. "Alexis and Alaina had been content to let the past be, as I was, but I figured when you finally learned the truth, you'd probably do something rash. I wanted to at least have an idea of who these people are, what they might do if you suddenly showed up."

"They're wonderful people," she said quietly. "They treated me with warmth and kindness and I responded with lies." She looked at Sam, then Clair. "I'm sorry. I'm so sorry."

"Kiera." Trey took her arm. "We should go now."

Sam moved forward, but before he could speak Clair

held out a hand to stop everyone. "No, please. Just stay the night here, at the Four Winds. We'll talk again, in the morning, when we've all had some rest."

"I appreciate the offer." Trey nodded stiffly at Clair. "But it's not necessary."

"For God's sake, Trey," Sam said through clenched teeth. "Can't you see Kiera's exhausted?"

"I don't need you telling me what my sister is." But he looked at her, saw the truth in her pale cheeks, and Trey's resolve took a hit. "Fine, we'll go back to your motel."

"I already checked out." She rubbed at the increasing pain in her head. "My bags are in my car."

"We'll find another place, then."

"Not at this hour you won't." Sam stepped in front of Trey. "Dammit, stop being an ass and think about Kiera."

Murder threatened in Trey's narrowed eyes. "Get the hell out of my way, Prescott, or we'll take this outside."

"I'll take it anywhere you want, Blackhawk." Sam stiffened, obviously preparing himself for another blow. "You want to go a few rounds, I'll be happy to oblige. Just let Kiera get some rest before she falls over."

"Stop it!" Kiera couldn't bear to see the two men she loved taking shots at each other. She laid a hand on her brother's chest, though it might as well have been a brick wall. "He's right, Trey," she said, lowering her voice. "It's too late to find a place to stay, and I am tired. Clair, if you're sure it's all right…"

"I'll call Housekeeping." Clair glanced at everyone in the room, then shook her head in disbelief. "We'll have breakfast in the morning and talk again, after we've all had a chance to sleep on this. Trey, if you come with me, I'll get you a key and have your luggage brought up."

"I can get my own luggage, thank you." Trey's jaw tightened when he looked at Sam. "Come on, Kiera—"

Kiera shook her head. "Go with Clair, Trey. Please."

He hesitated, then reluctantly followed Clair out of the room, but not before curling a lip at Sam. Unblinking, Sam didn't budge.

With a soft click, Clair closed the door behind her and Trey. The quiet of the room pounded in her skull, and she wished they were in the dark again. She steadied herself, tightly gripped the last thread of control and faced Sam.

He stood no more than three feet away, and she felt as if he might as well be on the other side of the world.

"I didn't want you to find out this way," she said softly.

"You didn't want me to find out at all."

Anger gripped his voice. After the lies and the deception, it was no less than she deserved. "I thought I could come here, find out about my father, who he was, why he'd left us. I was so certain that once I knew, I could let it go and move on with my life."

"Is that what you're going to do now?" Sarcasm laced with the anger. "Move on?"

"My job in Paris starts in three days. If I can get a flight tomorrow, I'll have just enough time to get settled in."

"So that's it, then?" he said through clenched teeth. "Now that you found out what you came here for, you can just walk away?"

She wanted to reach out to him, needed him to understand what she was feeling. But she couldn't, didn't dare touch him. Knew if she did, she would never want to let go. In spite of the cold shame sweeping through her, she held her voice even. "My father was a racist and maliciously ripped a family apart. He brought Clair and Rand and Seth nothing but pain. How could they ever look at me and not be reminded of that?"

"You don't give the Blackhawks enough credit." He bit the words out. "They've rebuilt their lives and each one of them is stronger because of it, more determined to make each and every day count."

"All the more reason for me to leave them alone." *To leave you alone,* she thought, and felt the pain squeeze her heart. "I'm sorry I came here, sorry I brought more heartache, but I'm not sorry about you, Sam. I know how you must feel, how you—"

He moved so fast she never saw it coming, and his hands were gripping her arms.

"You don't know a damn thing." He nearly lifted her off the floor. "You blow through here, deceive everyone, then think you can just blow out again and everything will be fine?"

"I—I'm sorry." The crazed look in his eyes caught her off guard. She struggled to breathe, to even think. "That's not what I meant."

"You come here, jump into my bed—"

"I did *not* jump." The anger felt good, so much better than the pain.

"The hell you didn't. You made me want you, dammit, and I didn't *want* to want you. All along, I knew you were hiding something, and still I wanted you." He let go of her so quickly, she stumbled back. "You want to run again, fine, then run. You do it so well."

Numb, she stared at him, felt the ice slowly form around her heart. How had it come to this? she thought dimly, closing her hands into fists so she wouldn't reach out to him, beg him to forgive her.

She loved him, and that would be her punishment, she realized. Because she would always love him, would always remember every minute of every day they'd spent together.

Somehow she managed to lift her chin and meet his angry gaze. Somehow she even managed to say goodbye.

And somehow she managed to turn and walk out the door.

Twelve

Standing at his office window, Sam watched the dawn slowly lift the darkness of the night. The courtyard and pool below were empty, the surrounding walkways damp from the early morning sprinklers. Overhead lights flickered off, and the distant roll of thunder promised a summer storm.

Just another day, he thought, watching the sun rise higher through the gathering clouds. Just another god-damned day.

He'd have to shower before he made rounds and greeted guests, of course. He rubbed a hand over his face, felt the stubble of his beard against his palm. He couldn't very well greet guests looking as if someone had just died.

Looking as if his heart was bleeding right out of his chest.

He'd stayed in his office after Kiera had walked out last night. He'd contemplated a visit to the bar, but chose to lick his wounds in private, rather than wash them down with an audience. He assumed everyone would know soon enough about Kiera. Who she was, who her father was. Tongues would be wagging from one end of Wolf River all the way to the next county, and the name William Blackhawk would once again be whispered in grocery store aisles and beauty salon chairs.

Who didn't love a good scandal?

He'd stood here all night, wondering how the hell he'd missed it so completely. He ran the past two weeks through his mind, over and over, then over again. There'd been clues, he could see that now, and Clair was right, there'd been something familiar about Kiera. But he'd been blind from the first moment he'd laid eyes on her.

Blind and stupid.

He glanced at his watch, considered a quick visit to the gym, thought maybe he could sweat off some of his frustration. But he wouldn't be alone. Even at this early hour there would be at least two or three guests and maybe a couple of employees in there. And with the mood he was in, he didn't trust himself to even be in the same room with another person without biting their head off.

For good measure, and just because he couldn't stop himself, he kicked his desk chair, watched it fly across the room and crash into a tall ficus tree. Dirt spilled from the heavy pot and a few loose leaves drifted to the floor.

Sure, he thought, *take it out on office furniture and potted plants.*

He should be thanking Kiera for leaving, he told

himself. If she'd stayed, he might have considered something exclusive with her, maybe something long-term.

Something permanent.

The thought turned his throat to dust. He'd spent a lifetime avoiding these kind of complications. He'd flown free as an eagle, not a damn care in the world. And then she'd walked into his life, and like a sparrow, he'd flown smack dab into a plate-glass window.

He was still dazed, still dusting himself off, and the bitter taste of her goodbye lodged tightly in his throat. He'd get over her, he told himself, gritting his teeth. Like her, he'd move on.

"You look like hell."

He glanced up sharply, saw Clair standing in the doorway. Dressed in a freshly pressed blue work suit, she looked crisp and new as the morning sun. He sighed heavily when he saw Dillon and Jacob were with her.

"Reinforcements?" he asked.

"Friends." She moved into the room, glanced at the chair tipped on its side and the spilled dirt. "You look like you could use a couple."

"Looks are deceiving, Clair." He frowned at the two men. "But we already know that, don't we? How's it feel to learn you have a sister, Dillon? Three actually, according to Kiera, and of course, there's Trey. With his dazzling charm, I'm sure you'll both be buds in no time."

With a sigh, Clair looked at Dillon and Jacob. "What did I tell you?"

"He's got it pretty bad, all right," Dillon said with a nod. "Don't you think so, Jacob?"

"Big-time." Jacob slipped an arm around his wife's shoulders. "I was there myself a few months ago, wasn't I, darlin'?"

"Me, too." Dillon nodded, his expression etched with pity. "Not a pretty sight, is it?"

"What the hell are you all talking about?" Sam barely kept his voice in check. He'd always liked these two men, but he was quickly changing his mind. "So maybe I had a thing for Kiera, but dammit I don't like being lied to. And why the hell are you all in such a damn good mood? She lied to you, too."

"I suppose she did," Clair said. "For all the right reasons, though. I know what it feels like, Sam. I was one of William's innocent victims, just like Kiera. Don't be angry with her. She needed the truth, but she's still reeling from it. Give her some time."

"We haven't *got* any time, dammit." He did yell now, felt the insanity explode inside him. "She's moving on, going to Paris. What the hell am I supposed to do about that?"

"Well, I'm not sure." Clair glanced from Dillon to Jacob. "You boys got any suggestions?"

"Far from me to interfere," Dillon said with a shrug.

"Wouldn't dream of it." Jacob shook his head and scratched the back of his neck. "But we did see her step into the elevator with her brother a few minutes ago. Looked like they had their luggage with them."

The smell of daylilies and roses filled the lobby of the Four Winds Hotel. The bouquet, a lush, five-foot-tall spray of fresh flowers on a wide, round glass table, brightened up the room and welcomed guests as they entered the hotel.

And as they left.

Her chest aching, Kiera stood by the arrangement, hoping it might somehow shield her from the pain of leaving. How strange it was that she'd lived in six different states, worked in eight large, cosmopolitan cities, but here, in Wolf River, was the one place where she'd felt as if she belonged. Bittersweet, she thought, which made her think of chocolate, which made her think of the soufflé she'd made for Sam.

But then, everything made her think of Sam.

A roll of thunder rattled the hotel windows.

She'd tried not to think about him. Even as she called a few minutes ago and left a message for Clair that they wouldn't be able to join her for breakfast, she'd been thinking of Sam, about how much she'd miss him. She told herself that once she got to Paris she would be so busy she wouldn't have time to think about him. She had a wonderful adventure ahead of her, living in Paris, working with a famous chef. It was a dream come true.

Surely the pain would ease with time, she told herself. Time and distance, and a demanding, busy work schedule.

She watched a couple walk off the elevator, holding hands and smiling, and the crack in her heart widened.

Oh, hell. Who was she lying to now? Time and distance wouldn't make one bit of difference. She would always love him, and somehow she'd simply have to learn to live with the pain of losing him.

She blinked back the moisture in her eyes, remembered the first time she'd seen him, watching her in that elevator, and she'd known at some instinctive level that they would be together. He'd been right about one thing, she thought dismally. She *had* jumped into his bed. And she'd do it again in a heartbeat. She loved him, maybe she'd loved him from that first moment, before she'd even seen his face. Maybe even before, if she believed in that sort of thing.

Which, unfortunately, she did.

So now here she stood, her overnight bag at her feet, waiting while her brother flustered the pretty blond desk clerk, who'd been told that the room Trey wanted to pay for had been comped. Trey, stubborn creature that he was, insisted he be given a bill. The poor girl had no idea what to do but had been on the phone for five minutes, obviously trying to locate the reservations manager.

He'd let her have her space last night after they'd got to their suite. As much as her brother loved a good fight, for once, thank God, he'd backed off. Even this morning, the only thing he'd said to her was, "I called the car rental company and made arrangements for them to pick your car up here at the hotel. I'll drive you to the airport."

Any other time, she might have argued with him. But she was coherent enough, barely, to know that he was right. If she got behind the wheel of a car in her current state of mind, there was no doubt she'd end up in a ditch somewhere. She understood that was how Trey showed his love—by taking control. They'd had a lifetime battle over the issue. She supposed they always would.

But just before they'd walked out of the suite, he'd stopped, then pulled her into his arms and held her tightly. Displays of tenderness were rare with her brother, and the unexpected hug threatened to unravel the loose threads barely holding her together. And yet, as the same time, she drew strength from his closeness.

She'd been angry with Trey for hiding the truth from her, but, in his own way, she understood that he'd only wanted to protect her. She'd forgive him for that—eventually. But could she forgive herself for all the grief she'd brought to Clair and the other Blackhawks?

And would they ever be able to forgive her?

Would Sam ever forgive her?

"You ready?"

She turned, saw Trey standing beside her. His dark eyes skimmed over her face.

"Yes."

"Why don't you wait here while I go get the truck?" He took her bag. "It's starting to rain."

She watched him walk through the glass double doors and head for the front parking lot. Lightning flashed, then thunder rumbled, stronger this time, and the sky suddenly opened. How appropriate, she thought with a sigh, and spotted Trey's truck behind two other cars pulling in to valet. Her pulse quickened, knowing he'd be here any minute and she'd really be leaving.

She glanced around the hotel lobby one more time. Everything looked so perfect here, so in sync. Felt so right. Knees wobbling, she headed for the doors.

The doorman smiled and stepped forward. "Good morning, Miss Kiera. Going to brave the storm?"

Kiera stopped and looked at the man, knew his name

was Joseph. *Going to brave the storm?* She glanced at the pouring rain and black sky outside, thought that it was nothing compared to the storm inside her.

Going to brave the storm?

Was she?

Or, like Sam had said, was she going to run away?

"Are you all right?" Joseph asked, frowning.

"No," she whispered. "I—I don't think I am."

A blast of air from outside swept around her. She stared at Trey's truck, pulling up out front, then back at Joseph.

"Is there anything I can do for you?" the doorman asked.

"No," she said, staring at the man. "I think I need to do it myself."

Lightning flashed when she spun on her heels; she felt the electricity rushing over her skin. She ran to the elevators, pushed the button several times and jumped inside when the doors finally opened. A tiny, gray-haired lady stepped inside with her. Kiera pushed the sixth-floor button at least three times.

"Com' on, com' on," she murmured, dancing from one foot to the other. *Isn't this just like me?* she thought. Impulsive and impatient? *Won't I ever learn?* She gave the door close button a solid smack. "Hurry."

"Bladder?" the woman asked politely.

Laughter bubbled in Kiera's throat and she shook her head. "A man."

"Oh." The old woman gave a knowing nod, then smacked the button herself. Biting her lip, Kiera watched the doors close.

A hand slipped in between the last sliver of space,

stopping the doors from closing. *No,* Kiera wanted to yell, almost did.

Until Sam stepped inside.

Breath held, she stared at him. He stared back, his eyes glassy and narrowed with determination.

The doors closed behind them.

His suit and tie were wrinkled, his hair messy and he definitely needed a shave. She thought he'd never looked better.

"You're not leaving." He worked a muscle in his jaw. "I won't let you."

"Sam—"

"Don't say a word, dammit." He pushed a button to stop the elevator. "Now it's your turn to be quiet and listen."

She bit her cheek, willed every muscle in her body to be still.

"I watched my mother marry and divorce half a dozen times," he began. "She kept shoes longer than she kept husbands. By the time I was twelve, I didn't even bother to remember their names, I just assigned them a number."

Sam dragged a hand through his already tousled hair. "They were all decent enough guys, except for Number Five. He turned mean after he lost a job, started drinking and one night he took out his frustration and anger on my mother. I walked in right after he'd used his fist on her. I was sixteen at the time, big for my age. They took him away in an ambulance that night and he became ex–Number Five."

She thought about the black eye she'd had when he'd first seen her. What he must have thought, what he would have felt. Shame filled her. "And I let you believe that about me, that I'd been in that kind of relationship."

"You told me the truth about that, but I still made an assumption. I shouldn't have. Now will you just let me talk?"

She pressed her lips firmly together, wished he would hurry.

"I joined the Army when I was eighteen," he continued. "Right after she married Number Six. I was in for four years, decided to get an education when I got out and put myself through college moonlighting at hotels. I liked living in different places, liked not having roots. Liked being able to move on whenever I felt like it."

When he paused, she started to speak again, but he put his fingertips on her mouth. "I never wanted to get married, never wanted a family, didn't think I'd make a good father, considering my lack of role models. I figured my brothers and sisters could give my mom grandkids."

"Brothers and sisters?" She could barely stop herself from kissing the fingers he still held to her lips.

"I have three sisters and two brothers," he said. "I'm the oldest."

She raised an eyebrow. "*That's* why you're so bossy."

He traced her lips with his index finger. "I don't care about your father. What he did or who he was. I don't care you hid your past from me. The only thing that matters, the only thing I care about, is you, Kiera Blackhawk."

It was the first time she'd ever heard him say her name, her real name, and the sound of it, the thrill, swam through her. She gazed up at him, wanted to tell him how she felt, that she loved him, but she couldn't find the words.

A hard glint narrowed his eyes. "You want to go to Paris, fine. We'll go together. They have hotels in Paris. Lots of them. I'll go to China, if you want, dammit. But don't leave." He grabbed hold of her shoulders. "Don't leave me."

He dropped his mouth on hers, kissed her urgently, then barely lifted his lips from hers. "Marry me."

Her heart stuttered. She stared at him, the emotion, her love for him, overwhelming her. "You—you want me to marry you?"

"Now." He tightened his grip on her arms. "Today. Tomorrow. Whenever you want, as long as it's soon. I'm not letting you go, not again. Dammit, Kiera, will you say something?"

She tried, she really did, but her throat had swelled with tears of joy.

"Might help if you tell her you love her," a tiny voice echoed in the elevator.

Sam turned his head sharply, saw the elderly woman watching them. Surprise clearly registered on his face, but he was a man on a mission and refused to be distracted, even by an audience. He glanced back at Kiera.

"I love you." He leveled his gaze with hers. "God help me, I love you."

"I love you, too." She reached out, touched his cheek, felt the stubble of his beard tingle up her arm. "I was coming back to tell you."

"You weren't leaving?"

She shook her head. "Not without telling you how I feel, without giving us a chance. Even if you turned me away, I had to know. If I decided to stay in Wolf

River, I knew I could face anything as long as you were by my side."

"I'd like to see you get rid of me." He kissed her again, with a tenderness that made tears flow. "Say yes, Kiera. Say you'll marry me. That you'll love me and have my babies."

Babies, she thought, as in *plural,* and her head spun. Until this minute, she hadn't realized how much she wanted babies. *Sam's* babies.

"Yes," she whispered, sliding her arms around his neck. "Yes to all of the above. *Yes.*"

This time when he kissed her, neither one of them heard the elevator doors open, or noticed that their audience had grown.

"This family keeps getting bigger by the minute," Dillon said to Clair.

With a wistful smile, Clair looped an arm through Dillon's, then leaned back against Jacob's broad chest. "Isn't it wonderful?"

"Best damn elevator ride I ever took." Clutching her purse to her heart, the gray-haired woman walked off the elevator.

"What the hell—"

At the sound of Trey's angry voice, Sam lifted his mouth from Kiera's and frowned. "We're getting married, Blackhawk. Deal with it."

Trey frowned back and stepped to the elevator, stared hard at Sam. "You break her heart, I'll break your legs." He stuck out his hand. "Welcome to the family."

The two men shook hands, then Sam punched the close doors button again. "Tell me you love me again," he murmured, pulling her into his arms after the doors closed.

"I love you, Sam Prescott." Smiling, she pushed the button for the sixth floor, then slid her hands up his arms. "I love you, I love you."

"Tell me you'll marry me." He brushed his lips over hers.

"There you go again, bossing me around." But she tightened her arms around his neck and pressed her lips to his. "I'll marry you, Sam Prescott. Today, tomorrow. Any day you say."

He kissed her, lingered over her soft, sweet lips while the elevator steadily climbed to the top floor. He figured that Clair and Jacob could handle any hotel problems for at least an hour. Maybe even two. "Tell me you'll make chocolate soufflé every day for the rest of our lives."

Laughing, she tossed her head back and looked into his eyes. "That would be boring."

The elevator doors opened and he scooped her into his arms, nibbled on her ear while he carried her down the hallway. "Darlin'—" he murmured, kissing her again when they were inside his suite "—of all the things I can be sure of, nothing about our life together will ever be boring."

* * * * *

Don't miss the next book in
Barbara McCauley's SECRETS! *series,*
available in December from Silhouette Desire.

A special treat for you from Harlequin Blaze!

Turn the page for a sneak preview of
DECADENT
by
New York Times *bestselling author*
Suzanne Forster

Available November 2006,
wherever series books are sold.

Harlequin Blaze—Your ultimate destination
for red-hot reads.
With six titles every month, you'll never guess
what you'll discover under the covers...

RUN, ALLY! Don't be fooled by him. He's evil. Don't let him touch you!

But as the forbidding figure came through the mists toward her, Ally knew she couldn't run. His features burned with dark malevolence, and his physical domination of everything around him seemed to hold her like a net.

She'd heard the tales. She knew all about the Wolverton legend and the ghost that haunted The Willows, an elegant old mansion lost by Micha Wolverton nearly a hundred years ago. According to folklore, the estate was stolen from the Wolvertons, and Micha was killed, trying to reclaim it. His dying vow was to be reunited with the spirit of his beloved wife, who'd taken her life for reasons no one would speak of, except in whispers.

But Ally had never put much stock in the fantasy. She didn't believe in ghosts.

Until now—

She still didn't understand what was happening. The figure had materialized out of the mist that lay thick on the damp cemetery soil. A cool breeze and silvery moonlight had played against the ancient stone of the crypts surrounding her, until they joined the mist, causing his body to thicken and solidify right before her eyes. That was when she realized she'd seen this man before. Or thought she had, at least.

His face was familiar. . . so familiar, yet she couldn't put it together. Not with him looming so near. She stepped back as he approached.

"Don't be afraid," he said. His voice wasn't what she expected. It didn't sound as if it were coming from beyond the grave. It was deep and sensual. Commanding.

"Who are you?" she managed.

"You should know. You summoned me."

"No, I didn't." She had no idea what he was talking about. Two minutes ago, she'd been crouching behind a moss-covered crypt, spying on the mansion that had once been The Willows, but was now Club Casablanca. And then this—

If he was Micah, he might be angry that she was trespassing on his property. "I'll go," she said. "I won't come back. I promise."

"You're not going anywhere."

Words snagged in her throat. "Wh-why not? What do you want?"

"If I wanted something, Ally, I'd take it. This is about need."

His words resonated as he moved within inches of her. She tried to back away, but her feet were useless. "And you need something from me?"

"Good guess." His tone burned with irony. "I need lips, soft and surrendered, a body limp with desire."

"My lips, my bod—?"

"Only yours."

"Why? Why me?" This couldn't be Micha. He didn't want any woman but Rose. He'd died trying to get back to her.

"Because you want that, too," he said.

Wanted what? A ghost of her own? She'd always found the legend impossibly romantic, but how could he have known that? How could he know anything about her? Besides, she'd sworn off inappropriate men, and what could be more inappropriate than a ghost? She shook her head again, still not willing to admit the truth. But her heart wouldn't play along. It clattered inside her chest. The mere thought of his kiss, his touch, terrified her. This wildness, it was fear, wasn't it?

When his fingertips touched her cheek, she flinched, expecting his flesh to be cold, lifeless. It was anything but that. His skin was smooth and hot, gentle, yet demanding. And while his dark brown eyes were filled with mystery and wonder, there was a sensitivity about them that threatened to disarm her if she looked too deeply.

"These lips are mine," he said, as if stating a universal fact that she was helpless to avoid. In truth, it was just that. She couldn't stop him.

And she didn't want to.

* * * * *

Find out how the story unfolds in...
DECADENT
by
New York Times *bestselling author*
Suzanne Forster.
On sale November 2006.

Harlequin Blaze—Your ultimate destination
for red-hot reads.
With six titles every month, you'll never guess
what you'll discover under the covers...

REQUEST YOUR FREE BOOKS!

2 FREE NOVELS PLUS 2 FREE GIFTS!

Silhouette®

Desire®

Passionate, Powerful, Provocative!

YES! Please send me 2 FREE Silhouette Desire® novels and my 2 FREE gifts. After receiving them, if I don't wish to receive any more books, I can return the shipping statement marked "cancel." If I don't cancel, I will receive 6 brand-new novels every month and be billed just $3.80 per book in the U.S., or $4.47 per book in Canada, plus 25¢ shipping and handling per book and applicable taxes, if any*. That's a savings of almost 15% off the cover price! I understand that accepting the 2 free books and gifts places me under no obligation to buy anything. I can always return a shipment and cancel at any time. Even if I never buy another book from Silhouette, the two free books and gifts are mine to keep forever.

225 SDN EEXJ 326 SDN EEXU

Name	(PLEASE PRINT)	
Address		Apt.
City	State/Prov.	Zip/Postal Code

Signature (if under 18, a parent or guardian must sign)

Mail to Silhouette Reader Service™:

IN U.S.A.	IN CANADA
P.O. Box 1867	P.O. Box 609
Buffalo, NY	Fort Erie, Ontario
14240-1867	L2A 5X3

Not valid to current Silhouette Desire subscribers.

Want to try two free books from another line?

Call 1-800-873-8635 or visit www.morefreebooks.com.

* Terms and prices subject to change without notice. NY residents add applicable sales tax. Canadian residents will be charged applicable provincial taxes and GST. This offer is limited to one order per household. All orders subject to approval. Credit or debit balances in a customer's account(s) may be offset by any other outstanding balance owed by or to the customer. Please allow 4 to 6 weeks for delivery.

SDES06

nocturne™

USA TODAY bestselling author

MAUREEN CHILD

ETERNALLY

He was a guardian. An immortal fighter of evil,
out to destroy a demon, and she was his next
target. He knew joining with her would make
him strong enough to defeat any demon.
But the cost might be losing the woman
who was his true salvation.

On sale November, wherever books are sold.

SAVE UP TO $30! SIGN UP TODAY!

INSIDE Romance

The complete guide to your favorite
Harlequin®, Silhouette® and Love Inspired® books.

✓ Newsletter ABSOLUTELY FREE! No purchase necessary.

✓ Valuable coupons for future purchases of Harlequin,
   Silhouette and Love Inspired books in every issue!

✓ Special excerpts & previews in each issue. Learn about all
   the hottest titles before they arrive in stores.

✓ No hassle—mailed directly to your door!

✓ Comes complete with a handy shopping checklist
   so you won't miss out on any titles.

- -

SIGN ME UP TO RECEIVE INSIDE ROMANCE
ABSOLUTELY FREE
(Please print clearly)

Name

Address

City/Town	State/Province	Zip/Postal Code

(098 KKM EJL9)

Please mail this form to:
In the U.S.A.: Inside Romance, P.O. Box 9057, Buffalo, NY 14269-9057
In Canada: Inside Romance, P.O. Box 622, Fort Erie, ON L2A 5X3
<u>OR</u> visit http://www.eHarlequin.com/insideromance

IRNBPA06R   ® and ™ are trademarks owned and used by the trademark owner and/or its licensee.

HARLEQUIN®

Blaze

New York Times bestselling author
Suzanne Forster brings you
another sizzling romance...

Club Casablanca—an exclusive gentleman's club where
exotic hostesses cater to the every need of high-stakes
gamblers, politicians and big-business execs. No rules
apply. And no unescorted women are allowed. Ever.
When a couple gets caught up in the club's hedonistic
allure, the only favors they end up trading are sensual....

DECADENT

November 2006

by

Suzanne Forster

Get it while it's hot!

Available wherever series romances are sold.

"Sex and danger ignite a bonfire of passion."
—*Romantic Times BOOKclub*

COMING NEXT MONTH

#1759 THE EXPECTANT EXECUTIVE—Kathie DeNosky
The Elliotts
An Elliott heiress's unexpected pregnancy is the subject of high-society gossip. Wait till the baby's father finds out!

#1760 THE SUBSTITUTE MILLIONAIRE—Susan Mallery
The Million Dollar Catch
What is a billionaire to do when he discovers the woman he's been hiding his true identity from is carrying his child?

#1761 BEDDED *THEN* WED—Heidi Betts
Marrying his neighbor's daughter is supposed to be merely a business transaction…until he finds himself falling for his convenient wife.

#1762 SCANDALS FROM THE THIRD BRIDE—
Sara Orwig
The Wealthy Ransomes
Bought by the highest bidder, a bachelorette has no recourse but to spend the evening with the man who once left her at the altar.

#1763 THE PREGNANCY NEGOTIATION—Kristi Gold
She is desperate to get pregnant. And her playboy neighbor is just the right man for the job.

#1764 HOLIDAY CONFESSIONS—
Anne Marie Winston
True love may be blind…but can it withstand the lies between them?